"There's nothing to talk about, Ashley," Stoner said. "I split open a white man's skull and it took eighteen stitches to close it back up. Ain't too much hope for a black man that's got this kind of trouble facing him."

"But Mr. Rucker provoked you, Daddy," Ashley said sharply. "You went out of your mind for a minute."

"You think an all-white jury's gonna understand how I felt when I saw that helpless old man fall in a heap at the bottom of the steps?" Stoner said. "No!"

That evening at the supper table Ashley watched Stoner pushing his biscuit through the molasses on his plate, a faraway look in his eyes. And Bessie kept excusing herself from the table to go mop away the tears that were welling up in her eyes.

THE LISTENING SKY

Bernice Anderson Poole

ISBN: 1-4922-6728-7
ISBN-13: 9781492267287

*To my daughters,
Trena, Scarlet, and Sonia.*

THE LISTENING SKY

Chapter 1

When Ashley Brooks opened his eyes dawn was breaking. He had overslept. He should have been at Mr. Peterson's house by now. They were going down to the river today to cut a load of wood and haul it back on the pickup. Ashley had lain awake half the night worrying about the trouble his father was in. The thought of his father going to prison for life tore at his insides like a vise.

Ashley was eighteen and had recently finished twelfth grade at the three-room school. He was a black boy facing the problems of growing up dirt poor in an environment of ignorance—ignorance among both whites and blacks.

Ashley lay on his back for a few minutes, listening to the crickets still droning outside. The small window next to his bed inhaled sweet morning air. How he dreaded getting up, but he desperately needed those few extra dollars Mr. Peterson paid him. Now that his family's own crop of tobacco had been harvested, Ashley had time to help Mr. Peterson do odd jobs. He planned to save every penny he could toward a college education. He had set his sights on being a lawyer someday. He didn't know how he was going to manage it, but he was sure it was going to happen, especially now that his father was in all this trouble.

This trouble and the threat of his father going to prison for life only made Ashley's burning desire to become a lawyer more intense.

In Mason County, North Carolina, in that year of 1936, racial prejudice was rampant. It was unheard of for a black to become a lawyer, but Ashley Brooks believed he could defy the odds.

Ashley jumped out of bed and pulled on a white T-shirt and his old faded jeans. He sat down on the side of the bed to lace up his runover brogans. He was tall, bronze, and handsome. He peered through the gray dawn of morning at his image in the mirror and combed and parted his dark curly hair and stuck the comb in his back pocket.

The trouble his father was in outweighed everything, but it wasn't the only thing bothering Ashley. His grandmother had died recently and this had taken a lot out of him. Also, he was in a bit of trouble himself. The word was out that the Willis brothers were out to get him.

Ashley slipped on the gold wristwatch his parents had struggled and saved to buy for his graduation and headed for the kitchen, where his mother was fixing breakfast.

Dull lamplight shone from the kitchen door as Ashley moved through the dark hall of their quarters.

"Morning, Ma." Ashley said, coming into the kitchen and heading for the washstand.

Bessie turned sharply. "You leaving now?" Her hands were covered with flour as she stood kneading dough for the breakfast biscuits. "I'm just getting ready to slip the biscuits in the oven."

"Yeah. I got to go. I promised Mr. Peterson I'd be there by daybreak. We don't get that wood cut and hauled back before noon the heat'll be unbearable." He poured some water from the bucket on the washstand into a basin and stooped over it, washing his face in the cold well water, his hands going in little circles over his face. He took the white towel off the nail on the wall and dried his face and hands. "Daddy getting ready to go?"

"Yes," Bessie said, sighing heavily as she rolled the dough into balls and laid them on the baker. "He didn't sleep a wink last night, Ashley." She looked around at her son, a worried expression on her face. Their eyes met and held.

Ashley walked to the open door and looked out the screen door. Outside the lantern light bobbed and weaved in the dark morning as Stoner moved about hitching the mule to the wagon for his trip into town to see his lawyer again.

Bessie was standing at the stove, turning over the pork meat frying for breakfast. She hurried back and patted out the biscuits and slipped them into the oven. She was moving as fast as she could in hopes Ashley would be able to eat before he left.

Ashley was late, but he stood looking out the screen door until he saw his father coming toward the house. He moved aside as Stoner opened the screen door and walked in.

"You leaving now?" Stoner asked. He blew out the lantern and set it in the corner.

"I was waiting until you came in," Ashley said. Then he looked straight at Stoner and asked, "What time you supposed to be there?" He didn't like the haggard look on his father's face.

"Around ten," Stoner said. He was a big man. At eighteen he had looked exactly like Ashley. He began rolling back his shirtsleeves to wash up for breakfast. "If I leave right after breakfast, I'll make it there in plenty time."

"I was just thinking," Ashley said. "If you didn't have to be there until this evening, I could get Mr. Peterson's truck and run you to town after we finish with the wood."

"Ain't no need for that," Stoner said, drying his hands.

Ashley walked over and ladled up a drink of water in the long-handled metal dipper and drank. Not that he was thirsty; he was stalling, because he felt sorry for his father and wished he knew what to say to cheer him up.

Stoner sat down on the end of the long bench and rubbed his hand over his face.

Ashley put the dipper back in the bucket, his eyes on his father. "You gonna be all right?"

"I'm all right," Stoner said. Ashley turned to leave.

"You ain't got time to eat breakfast?"

Ashley looked at his watch. "Naw. I'm already thirty minutes late."

Bessie peeped at the biscuits. They were not done yet. If she could have performed a miracle and made the biscuits cook quicker she would have. Bessie was dark brown. She wore her short hair parted in the middle and cornrowed on each side. From all the farm work she still had her girlish figure, even after bearing three children. Ashley's two younger sisters were still asleep.

"Well, I'll see y'all this evening," Ashley said, turning to leave.

Bessie looked at Ashley's hair, parted and neatly combed. "Son, you need a hat on your head out there in that hot sun all day." She told Ashley this each time he went out to work, and each time he ignored her.

Ashley turned back to his father. "Daddy, you got to stop worrying so much. Mr. Taylor is the best lawyer anywhere around." Ashley paused. "And you ain't done no more'n no other black man would've done in a situation like that, seeing a white man shove an old black man down a flight of steps just 'cause he was asking for something that was rightly his."

Stoner looked thoughtfully across the room, perhaps remembering what had happened that day and feeling the excitement all over again.

Ashley walked back through the house. He peeped in the room where his two sisters lay sleeping. He usually teased them before he left, but they were sound asleep. He walked on past the door of the bedroom his grandmother had occupied for so long. He glanced at the bed made up neatly with the colorful quilt turned back at the foot, just as she always kept it. How he missed her.

Ashley ran most of the way to Mr. Peterson's house. As he came near, he stopped running and began to walk, taking long strides, allowing himself to think about his troubles once again. A million thoughts swirled in his head. The trouble his father was in weighed heavier on his mind than anything else, but Ashley had some trouble himself since the three Willis brothers had been out to get him.

Ashley glanced at his watch and moved a little faster toward the white house. He suddenly thought of John, Mr. Peterson's twelve-year-old son. The boy was sort of hard to handle. Ashley sure hoped he wouldn't be going with them. Ashley remembered the day he had almost cut John's head off. John had come along on a wood-cutting trip, and before they had begun work, he and John had been horsing around. Ashley had quit and started cutting wood. He had the axe swung high over his head, about to bring it down with all his might against the log, when John came bounding out of nowhere and grabbed him. Ashley had to think fast to keep the axe from striking John.

When Ashley got to Mr. Peterson's backyard he heard noises coming from the green pickup truck parked out by the tall pecan tree. John was sitting behind the wheel going, "Virrrrrrr, virrrrr, virrrr," pretending to drive the truck. When he saw Ashley his eyes lit up.

"Come on, jump in, Ashley. I'm driving you and

Pa down to the river." He grinned at Ashley.

Ashley leaned against the door. "Hey, man, you really do look like you know how to drive that thing."

"I do." John said. "Pa just won't let me. He only lets me drive the tractor."

The kitchen door opened and Peterson emerged carrying a red-and-white cooler and a large brown paper bag. Mrs. Peterson had packed them lemonade, a batch of ham sandwiches, and half a chocolate cake.

"Morning," Peterson said, walking toward the truck.

"Morning," Ashley replied. He stood there, waiting for John to get out.

Peterson walked around to the driver's side. "Come on and get out, son. We'd best get going." Peterson was a tall, wiry man, with piercing blue eyes and a thick crop of dark brown hair. He was munching on a plug of tobacco in his jaw. He spat across the white sandy yard, waiting for John to get out.

John set in begging to go. "Please, Pa. I'll behave myself. Please?"

"Son, I've already told you a thousand times. No!" Peterson opened the door ."I don't want you anywhere near that river."

John began crying and carrying on. Pretty soon his nose was running and his eyes were red.

John turned sad eyes on Ashley. "Ashley, please tell Pa to let me go!"

Ashley scoured his hand over the boy's head in sympathy.

"Goldernit, son, get on out of the truck!" Peterson said. He spat across the yard and wiped the back of his hand over his lips.

While Peterson and Ashley got into the truck, John kept carrying on, whining and pleading until finally Peterson gave in and told him that he could go along with them.

The pickup roared down the sandy path toward the river, its tires straining against the sand. John sat sandwiched between Peterson and Ashley, a happy glint in his eyes.

Soon they were creeping through a jungle-like thicket. Cold morning air rushed through the window. Birds that had been twittering in the treetops undisturbed stopped their morning song and took flight at the approach of the truck. A red fox peeped out of the thicket and then disappeared.

Peterson kept gunning the engine until they arrived at the area where a clump of oak trees stood. The trees were a nice size, not too big for them to handle. They would make good firewood. Ashley and Peterson often cut logs here and hauled them back to the house, where they cut them down into stove wood, which they took into town to sell to people, doing a good business.

Peterson parked the truck a safe distance from the river. Ashley hauled out the saw, and set to work on the first tree.

John had already strayed from the truck, exploring the territory. Peterson called him back twice. "Goldernit, son. I told you to stay close to us! Don't let me have to tell you that again!"

Then he scolded John for standing too close to the saw Ashley was operating. John moved back some, inch by inch, until he was in the woods out of sight of his father.

He was trying to get close enough to see the huge river that he knew loomed not too far away. He was yearning for just one glimpse of the mysterious body of water that he had been begging to see for as long as he could remember.

John had managed to get a good distance away, hidden in the woods, before he heard his father calling him. Then he tore through the bushes, back to where the truck was parked, before Peterson could realize how far he had strayed.

By noon, Ashley and Peterson had cut a truckload of logs and piled them on the pickup.

Peterson spread an old gunnysack on the ground and brought their lunch from the truck. They hauled out some sacks and the three of them sat down to eat. Earlier, Ashley's stomach had been grumbling, and the country-cured ham sandwiches, cold lemonade, and chocolate layer cake were delicious.

John ate as fast as he could and began playing nearby, plucking imbedded stones from the dark moist ground. He sailed them as high in the treetops as his chubby arm would send them. John had left his father and Ashley talking about a murder that had occurred in the county. They were almost done for the day and were in no hurry to go back to work.

John eyed his father as he rubbed his behind, which was cold and numb from sitting on the ground, and inched farther into the woods toward the river. He figured his father wouldn't notice he was gone.

Ashley and Peterson's conversation was about a white farmer in Mason County who had been shot and left alongside a lonely country road. They sat finishing eating now and talking about it. Some people said it was Tom Willis who had murdered the white farmer.

Tom Willis was the oldest of three brothers who went for bad. Of the three black brothers, Tom, Lewis, and Tank, only Tom was capable of murder. Everyone knew this. Lewis and Tank were of the misdemeanor type. Nonetheless, everyone in Mason County was intimidated by the Willis boys' frequent displays of preposterous behavior.

Now the Willis boys were out to get Ashley.

Ashley was on his third sandwich. Peterson was cutting the cake. He looked over at Ashley. "I hear Tom Willis shot that man because he slapped his brother Tank."

"I wouldn't doubt it," Ashley said. He suddenly lost his appetite at the mention of Tom Willis. "Tom's crazy. The boy needs to be put away." Ashley cleared his mouth of food. He found a tiny sharp twig and picked his teeth.

"Tom Willis and his brother Lewis are always defending Tank," Ashley said. "And Tank don't do nothing but start trouble."

Ashley paused, one leg stretched out, the other propped up. He hadn't really intended to tell Peterson, but the thing was bothering him some, so he went on and let it out. "Tom and Lewis are after me now," he said, looking over at Peterson, a smile playing at the corner of his lips.

Peterson was drinking lemonade. He brought the tin cup down from his mouth immediately, looking straight at Ashley.

"What happened?"

"Well...," said Ashley hesitantly. He threw out both hands. "I didn't want to get tangled up with their kind, Mr. Peterson. It just happened." Ashley looked off into the woods pensively, then repeated, "It just happened. Tank Willis pushed me just a little too far the other night when I was over at the Chicken Shack. He's always starting trouble and then depending on his brothers to bail him out."

He looked at Peterson, a frown line on his forehead. "Tank was messing with my friend. I just couldn't take it. I tried my level best to knock his damn head off!" Ashley said, his face as angry as he had felt when it had happened.

Peterson stared down at the ground thoughtfully. "If I were you, son, I'd stay away from their kind. They're not worth getting yourself in trouble for."

Ashley stared off in the distance. He didn't answer Peterson. He knew he was already in trouble. He was trying not to think about it, but the fact that crazy Tom Willis carried around a shotgun in his old beat-up car made him jittery.

John was out of sight of his father and Ashley. He stopped walking and listened to make sure he didn't hear his father calling him. Must have been the wind, he thought, making that wavering yoo-hoo sound. He walked on, cautiously peering ahead into the tangle of underbrush. That river just had to be somewhere nearby. He could smell it. It smelled like the string of fish his father brought home sometimes, the fishes' eyeballs bulging, a tree branch strung through their gills.

All John wanted to do was get one look at that body of water he had heard so much about, maybe throw a few stones in it. Hear that p-l-o-m-p sound they made when they hit the water.

John parted a clump of bushes and his eyes grew wide. There it lay! Huge, gray, and still. Still as death. He reached in his pocket and felt the stones he'd gathered, curling his fingers around the solidity of them. He inched on, whispering to himself in awe, "Wow! Look at that!"

It beckoned him, mesmerized him. He couldn't take his eyes off it. It was like the luscious chocolate cake his mother baked and left on the kitchen table for the icing to get firm, telling him not to touch it. The temptation was as strong as the need to rub a finger over the cake, get a glob of icing and wipe it across his tongue, and smack his lips.

John glanced at the handful of stones he held ready and began inching closer to the precipice overlooking the river. From the edge it was almost a straight drop down to the rushing water, with only a small ledge or outcropping of growth here and there.

He threw a stone with all his might, hoping to hear that p-l-o-m-p sound. It fell short. Didn't make a sound. He tried it again. This one went g-l-o-o-m-p! He grinned, marveling at the sound.

John suddenly realized he had gotten very close to the river's edge, and he turned to move away. But he stopped at the sight of a big snake coiled at his feet, aware at the same time that it was making a rattling sound. John cried out and, without thinking, stepped backwards over the precipice. Screaming frantically as he slid down the steep incline, he tore at the soft dirt with his fingernails to try to keep from plunging into the water, finally grabbing a small bush growing there. He clung to the bush for dear life, glancing wild-eyed at the threatening dark river that rushed and swirled a few feet down the slippery bank.

Peterson and Ashley were in the process of gathering up the leftovers and putting them back in the truck, still talking about the Willis boys. When they heard the bloodcurdling screams, their eyes met and immediately they knew what was happening!

Ashley made a quick dash across the clearing and tore through the woods like a bullet. Peterson followed, numb with fear.

Ashley ran through the thick underbrush like lightning, tree branches slapping his face and poking him in the ribs. Peterson moved as fast as he could, but the younger, more agile man beat him to the river.

When Ashley arrived at the river, he spotted John clinging to the small bush, crying, his eyes wild with fear. The bush was uprooting fast.

"Hang on, man!" Ashley yelled, tugging to remove his brogans.

John let out one last desperate scream as the bush uprooted and he plunged into the river, taking the bush with him. Ashley dove into the murky water, making a tremendous splash, just as Peterson arrived breathlessly. Ashley rose to the surface, gasping for breath and looking around for John. Ashley dove again.

Peterson stood frozen in terror on the bank, his face

white as a sheet. He couldn't swim, so he had to depend on Ashley to save his son. Glaring down at the dark water, he muttered, "My God! My God! Please save him!"

Ashley again rose to the surface, gulping air, but still without John. Immediately he went down again and this time popped up from the water with John in his arms. John was fighting him desperately, his choking sounds audible over the roar of the rushing water, but Ashley managed to get him under control.

Peterson stood with a frozen gaze as Ashley swam toward the bank, holding John's head above the surface and moving at an angle slightly downstream in order to conserve his strength. Peterson, his chest pounding with hope, ran along the riverbank shouting encouragement to Ashley. Finally reaching the edge of the river, Ashley shoved John's limp body out of the water onto a level piece of ground on the riverbank and then crawled onto the bank himself, breathing heavily and collapsing beside the boy.

However, Ashley knew he could not take time to rest. Though he had hardly any strength left, he rose to his knees and began giving John artificial respiration. Soon, about the time Peterson arrived at their side, John was coughing up the river water and regaining his breath.

The two men managed to get the boy up the incline away from the river. Then Ashley fell on the grass. He was exhausted and red-eyed.

Peterson sat cradling John's head, as if afraid to let his son out of his arms. After he had managed to regain his strength, Ashley got up and walked over to them and stood over them.

John stopped sniffling and crying and looked up at Ashley, still rather dazed and confused but obviously aware that Ashley had saved his life. Ashley rubbed his hand over the boy's head. John smiled weakly.

Peterson looked up at Ashley. "Thank you, son," he said gratefully. "Where in the world did you learn how to swim like that?" His deep blue eyes held passion and sincerity as he added, "I'll be in debt to you for the rest of my life for saving my boy."

When he walked home after work that evening, Ashley took his time, thinking about things. He had a lot to think about. However, his mind did not stay on his troubles, but instead his thoughts drifted to his grandmother.

Ashley had not gotten over the death of his grandmother. He recalled the many times her frail hands had reached out to caress his hands when he told her about problems he was having at school or in the community, with some boy who disliked him or was jealous of him.

Ashley thought of the time when he had been in first grade and had got a bloody nose from a fight. He had been sitting on the porch steps crying, when his grandmother came and sat down beside him and put her arm around him. She held him in her arms while he finished crying and then wiped his eyes.

She had explained to him that during his lifetime there would be many times when life wouldn't seem fair, when he would feel as if the whole world was against him. She confided to Ashley the solution she had used to deal with her own problems. "Ashley, son," she told him, holding him in her arms, her warm cheek against his wet cheek, "when you're troubled and need someone to talk to, look up and talk to the sky. God's always listening."

As Ashley walked back home now, recalling her advice, he glanced up at the sky. It looked so peaceful and serene, and somehow it made him feel the same. "Grandma," he muttered, smiling upward, "thank you."

It wasn't the first time he had reason to be grateful for his grandmother's wise counsel and advice. Grandma had been right about many things, but especially about the listening sky. Throughout his life, he had found comfort by looking up and talking silently to the sky. He now knew that it had been his grandmother's way of telling a young child how to pray, but because it was their own privately shared means of prayer it was all the more meaningful to Ashley.

As Ashley's steps took him nearer to home, his thoughts turned to his father. Stoner was hardworking, a strong believer in treating his fellow man as he wanted to be treated, but because of this latest trouble, Ashley wondered if his father's simple, peaceful days were over, days of walking behind the old mule in the field and plowing, feeling the good free dirt under his feet.

Ashley and his family lived on the Brinkley farm. They were tenant farmers, but Mr. Brinkley was a man who cared about people, black and white, and he was fair with the people on his place. Mr. Brinkley lived in the small town of Mason, but he visited his farms frequently to make certain things were running smoothly between the overseer and the farmers.

Thomas Rucker was the overseer for Mr. Brinkley, and he lived in the "big house" up the road from Ashley and his family. He was an efficient overseer. This was the reason Brinkley had kept him on, although he sometimes drank heavily. But lately the farmers had been complaining about Rucker's bad temper when he was drinking. A white farmer had Rucker up recently for throwing a hammer at him, which had barely missed his head. Rumor was spreading that Rucker was losing his mind. But now it was because of Rucker that Stoner was in trouble.

After supper that night, Ashley and his father went out and sat on the porch, talking about what had happened the day that Stoner had got himself in a world of trouble.

It was dusk dark. Fireflies flitted across the yard and out in the fields like jewels in the gray dark. Stoner and Ashley sat on the left side of the porch on a tattered old brown leather sofa they had dragged from inside the house some time ago. Occasionally, from down on the highway, the drone of a passing car would waft toward them.

"Usually I stayed away from him," Stoner said, meaning Thomas Rucker. "If I just hadn't gone up there that morning."

"I told you, Daddy, any black man would have reacted the same way!" Ashley said. "Mr. Rucker had no business shoving Mr. Sam down the steps. Old man like that, he could have killed him. All Mr. Sam want-

25

ed was what he had worked for. What was rightly his."

It was true that Stoner had stayed clear of Thomas Rucker, for Stoner himself had a quick temper. That Monday morning of the incident Stoner had gone up to the big house for fertilizer. He tied his mule to the china tree and when he started toward the house he heard loud voices. Rucker and Sam were standing on the back porch arguing about something.

Stoner didn't want to be there. He didn't want to overhear the argument. Mr. Sam was an elderly black man, too old for the fields, and he did odd jobs for Thomas Rucker around the big house.

Rucker had promised Sam one of his best hams for painting the kitchen. When Sam finished, Rucker refused to give him the ham, saying he hadn't promised him a ham at all, but only a piece of side meat.

Stoner, once again, reviewed the entire sequence of events for Ashley. He couldn't help talking about it. He wanted everyone to understand just how it had happened, so they would realize how his pride had been attacked, his manhood, which had left him no choice but to come to Mr. Sam's aid.

"When I looked, Mr. Rucker was waving his finger in Mr. Sam's face." Stoner said. "And that old man's black face was still wet with sweat from all the work he'd done. He had to scrape the peeling paint from the walls, patch up the cracks, then give it two good coats of paint."

"That was a lot of work," Ashley said. "Mr. Sam deserved a lot more than a ham for that."

"When I heard them arguing I stopped and leaned

against the tree and waited," Stoner said. "I could see and hear everything going on, though. I was right there close to the porch. I was hoping they would hurry and resolve the argument." Stoner went on to explain what happened.

Sam raked a finger across his forehead to wipe off the sweat streaming down his face. "But you did, Mr. Rucker. You said the minute I finished I could go get the ham from the smokehouse."

"Dammit, Sam, I said you could have a side of meat. Not one of my best hams!"

"Yes you did, Mr. Rucker. You said there was a right smart of work to be done, scraping, patching...." Had the man been drinking when he had promised him the ham? Sam had too much respect for him to ask that question.

The old man was tired, old and tired—tired of working like a dog all of his life, with nothing to show for it but a broken body. He had done a good job, taken pride in his work. Now he wanted his ham. He was tired of eating fatback. The thought of that country-cured ham, with red-eye gravy, molasses, and hot biscuits, must have seemed mighty appealing to the old man. Sam continued to try to refresh Rucker's memory.

"You can ask Mrs. Rucker," Sam said. "We were standing right here like we is now, and she was standing right over there."

When Sam pointed to where Mrs. Rucker had been standing, his finger came close to Rucker's nose by accident.

Rucker slapped at Sam's finger and missed.

"Dammit, Sam," he shouted, red-faced, "don't you ever put your black hand in my face!" He grabbed Sam, spun him around, and delivered a swift kick to his behind. Standing close to the edge of the porch near the steps, Sam lost his balance and went plummeting down five steps to the ground.

As Stoner told the story, his voice rose heatedly. It was obvious to Ashley just how angry the incident had made his father.

"When I saw that old man come tumbling down them steps and fall in a heap on the ground, something inside me exploded!" Stoner said.

"I know it did," Ashley said. He had felt the exact same way when his friend had been attacked. "I just can't stand to see somebody taken advantage of."

"I jumped up on that porch and hit him before I knowed what was happening," Stoner said.

When Stoner had slammed his fist against Rucker's head, knocking him backwards, Rucker's head had hit the corner of an old iron stove sitting on the porch, cutting a deep gash on his head. He lay bleeding profusely.

Scared as Stoner was after this happened, he jumped in Rucker's old pickup and rushed him to the hospital. It took eighteen stitches to close the gash in Rucker's scalp, and he was hospitalized for two weeks.

The sheriff of Mason County was called out to the Rucker place that day, and Stoner was arrested. Stoner had been released on bail, but his day in court was rapidly approaching.

Lately Rucker had been going around boasting

about how Stoner Brooks was going to be put away for a long time for assault and battery on a white man.

The whole mess was a nightmare for Stoner and his family, even though Mr. Brinkley had hired the best lawyer in Mason County for him, and they had been working on his defense. But best lawyer or not, Stoner had little hope of remaining a free man much longer.

There had been a similar situation some years back. A black farmer had beat his overseer for slapping his wife, and he was still serving time, with no chance for parole.

Chapter 2

A general store was to the country folk around Mason County what a supermarket was for the city folk. There was no limit to what one could buy in one of those funny—but delicious—smelling stores. The floor looked as if it had been greased with black oil, and in the summertime a fan whirred lazily in the ceiling; it was always dark and cool inside as the tenant farmers dropped in for a cold Pepsi and a pack of cheese nabs, a can of sardines or pork and beans, a slice of rich cheese, and a box of crackers for their lunch. If you had a pocketful of change, a visit to the general store could be like dying and going to heaven.

The front yard of Mr. Snellings's general store in Ashley's territory was a gathering place—both for grownups and teenagers—especially on Saturday afternoons after twelve, when everybody got off work, rushed home and cleaned up, and came back to the store for the sole purpose of making plans for the evening, especially Saturday night. Some got started on drinking sprees that lasted till Sunday night.

The poor country folk all wore the same sort of attire. The females had it a little better than the males, for their dresses could be home-sewed from brightly colored materials sold from bolts in the general store, if they could afford it, or made from flour-sack material.

The men wore mostly faded jeans and starched white shirts when they dressed up, the jeans thoroughly ironed and creased, and the shirts bleached and stiff-collared from starch. The ironing was usually done by the teenage girls in the families, using little black, flat irons heated on wood stoves. Sometimes the irons got too hot, and if one wasn't careful she left a big brown impression of the iron on a white shirt. The older women were experts at ironing, rarely making that mistake.

If the weather was cool the men wore the jackets to their one and only suit, which was kept hanging up behind the door and waiting for church once in awhile, or a funeral.

Tick and Bucky were good friends of Ashley's. They were standing outside Mr. Snellings's general store that Saturday afternoon. Tick was tall and as skinny as a pencil, and Bucky had a body like Joe Louis.

To the people of Mason County, and millions of other Negroes, Joseph Louis Barrow, born in rural

Alabama, where his parents themselves had been tenant farmers—better known as Joe Louis—was not only a great fighter but a symbol of hope for the Negro people.

Bucky and Tick, dressed like typical teenagers, were laughing and talking. Bucky was pouring his pack of peanuts into his Nehi grape soda when he turned to Tick, standing beside him up against Bucky's old Ford, and said "Hey, man, did you hear about Ashley saving Mr. Peterson's boy from drowning?"

Tick, skinning the wrapper off a Payday candy bar, said, "Yeah, I heard all 'bout it. You know Ashley. If he ain't getting somebody's cat out of a well or helping old ladies up and down the church steps, he's saving somebody from drowning."

Bucky turned his soda up to his mouth and caught and chewed a mouthful of soggy peanuts. "Thinks he's Joe Louis, too. The other night over at the Chicken Shack he flattened old Tank Willis because he kept picking on Melvin Sims."

"Yeah," Tick said. "Ashley's just like his old man. He can't stand to see somebody pick on somebody."

"I was glad Ashley busted that sucker in the mouth. He deserved it. If he hadn't done it I'd 'a' done it," Bucky said. "The only thing I hate is that Ashley didn't kick him in the ass after he knocked him down."

"I wish I'd 'a' been there," Tick said. "What'd Tank do when Ashley knocked him on his ass?"

"The son of a bitch was too scared to try to defend hisself," Bucky said. "He ain't shit without them crazy-ass brothers of his. After Ashley knocked him down he just lay there like he was dead till Ashley was long gone."

Tick threw back his head and let out a belly-whopping laugh, bending to his knees, and some white and Negro farmers who were standing around drinking together stopped talking and looked over at Bucky and Tick.

Bucky was about to take a drink from his soda, but Tick's hearty laughter tickled him and he spilled grape drink down the front of his white shirt. Luckily, because of all the starch, the soda rolled off in purple beads and didn't stain the fabric.

After Tick caught his breath he said, "I don't blame old Tank from laying there till Ashley left. That Ashley Brooks has got muscles like the man's on the Arm & Hammer soda box."

"Yeah," Bucky said, looking thoughtfully at the ground, "but I wouldn't want to see Ashley get hurt by Lewis or Tom Willis. You know how they are about their baby brother."

"Don't worry 'bout Ashley Brooks; he can take care of himself," Tick said.

"Yeah, but those muscles ain't no match for that old shotgun that Tom Willis carries around!" Bucky said. Then he pulled out a pack of Juicy Fruit chewing gum and opened it. Tick's hand was already waiting for a stick before Bucky offered him one.

"Let's ride over to the Chicken Shack and see what's happening," Bucky said.

Surrounded by tall, waving corn in the summertime and barren fields in the winter, the Chicken Shack was where the teenagers gathered to dance, socialize, and often skip out into the cornfields and make love. The barren fields in the wintertime allowed the blatant music of the jukebox to be heard as far around as the winter wind would carry it.

Bucky and Tick could hear the loud music as Bucky's old black Ford rolled up the dusty path toward the one-room shack.

The place was owned by a short, fat man named Joe Jones, whom everyone called "Mr. Five-by-Five" because he was almost as wide as he was tall. The white apron he always wore displayed orange, grape, and strawberry drink stains across the front. His forehead stayed studded with beads of sweat, especially in the summertime, when the place was like a hothouse. Joe especially enjoyed watching the girls spin around, waiting for their skirts to fly up so he could look for something.

Bucky had parked near the water pump and he and Tick were headed for the gray, weather-beaten building with their chests thrown back and their noses open for some Saturday evening fooling around.

Tick stopped suddenly and began using his handkerchief to rub the dust off his carefully spit-shined shoes. Bucky stopped to wait for him and pulled out his comb to give his hair a last minute touch-up.

"Ah, come on, man," he called to Tick. "Your shoes look good enough for old Ella Mae

Ella Mae was a girl that Tick didn't really like, but she was crazy about him and was easy to get.

Tick stopped rubbing his shoes and stood up. "Man, if Ruth comes tonight, you can have Ella Mae.

Ruth was Tick's girl.

"Don't do me no small favors, man," Bucky said. When Bucky and Tick walked in they could feel the vibrations of the dancing feet against the plank floor, making it pump up and down like heartbeats. The huge room was packed with laughing, chattering, and dancing teenagers.

Over in the corner of the room was a small area fenced in by a counter, where Joe sold cigarettes and refreshments. Joe was busy filling the drink box with warm drinks when Tick walked up to the counter and slapped it hard to get his attention. Joe looked around and smiled, happy as always to see friends.

"Whatcha know, Joe?" Tick said.

"Don't know nothing," Joe replied, as he always did whenever he was asked that. (The boys always greeted him that way.)

"Seen any pretty cunts lately?" Tick asked him.

"Sho have," Joe answered. "See that gal over there in the flare skirt?" Joe pointed out a girl to them. "Man, she's got the prettiest thighs you ever want to see; know she's got a pretty ass...uh, uh, make your mouth water; just watch her the next time she spins around."

Bucky and Tick peeled their eyeballs in the girl's direction, but to their disappointment, the fast-paced record went off and a slow one came on.

Bucky and Tick remained at the counter talking to Joe; then Bucky whispered to the other two, "There's Tank Willis over there. Think he's looking for Ashley?"

"No way," Tick said. "You don't see those mean son-of-a-bitch brothers with him, do you? Ashley

Brooks is the last man on earth that nigger wants to see, especially if his brothers aren't around."

They laughed.

Jasper Jones suddenly appeared in the crowd. Everyone knew Jasper for what he was: a liar, a gossiper, and a troublemaker. Wherever he went he found it imperative to start trouble if there was any way he possibly could.

Jasper had heard about Ashley's fight with Tank and was determined to stir in the situation as much as he possibly could; it was his reason for being there.

He walked up to Bucky, Tick, and Joe and leaned himself against the counter. His wide-brimmed winter hat was pressed down over his ears and sweat was running down in front of each ear. He smelled of sweat and strong cigarette smoke.

"I hear that Tom and Lewis are looking for Ashley to beat his goddamned ass, or maybe put a few buckshot in him, for fucking with their brother!" Jasper said.

Neither Joe, Bucky, nor Tick acknowledged his presence, but Joe had noticed Tom and Lewis Willis hanging around in the place for the past few nights since the fight, just long enough to look the place over for Ashley, he thought. Joe was afraid for Ashley and hoped he wouldn't come to the Chicken Shack until the whole mess had died down.

Jasper Jones realized that he was being totally ignored, so he left and went over to where Tank Willis was standing.

Tick slammed his fist against the counter. "I know that son of a bitch is trying to start something, I just know he is," he said to Bucky and Joe.

A slow record came on and the place quieted down some. The fast dancers were gathering around the counter, dripping sweat and ordering cold drinks.

Bucky and Tick left Joe and moved over toward where Melvin Sims and his girl, Patty, were standing. It was the first time either one of them had seen Melvin since Ashley had defended him against Tank Willis.

Patty was watching Melvin while he stooped to select her favorite record on the jukebox.

"Hi, Patty," Bucky said playfully, ignoring Melvin's presence. "I do believe you get prettier with each day that passes." She smiled and Melvin looked up and smiled. Neither of them mentioned the fight.

The fight had taken place a few nights before. Ashley had noticed Tank trying to force Patty to dance with him. Tank had grabbed Patty's arm on several occasions and she had literally fought him off. Ashley knew that Melvin was no fighter and that Tank wouldn't rest until he'd challenged him to the point of fighting to protect his girl. When Melvin had taken all he could of Tank's irrational behavior, he had told Tank to stop putting his hands on his girl. Tank had grabbed Melvin by the collar and ordered him to follow him outside.

Tank had marched outside, thinking Melvin was following him, but when he turned to swing at Melvin, he was facing Ashley Brooks. Before he could duck his head, Ashley's hard fist had leveled him to the ground and he lay wiping blood from his busted lip.

A fast record came on and the floor crowded up

again with fast dancers. Bucky and Tick noticed that Jasper had gone back over to the counter and was trying to talk to Joe. They hurried back to the counter to see what he was saying.

"That Ashley Brooks sho better watch his step," Jasper was saying when Bucky and Tick walked up. "That Tom and Lewis Willis are the two meanest cats I know! Did you know that Tom killed a man once for messing with Tank!" Bucky looked at Tick and Tick at him. "They say that Ashley Brooks is just like his old man. Did you all hear 'bout Stoner Brooks knocking the hell out that white man?"

Jasper again was completely ignored, so he walked away. Joe, Bucky, and Tick watched him drift over to the jukebox, then suddenly make a beeline to the two Willis brothers, who had just walked in. Tom Willis was looking the entire place over with his bloodshot eyes. The place got very quiet. All eyes were on Tom, knowing he was looking for Ashley.

There they were—the three Willis brothers, who always cast a shadow on a room, and Jasper Jones, the shit-stirring heller—bringing the fun to a standstill.

"You see that?" Tick said to Bucky and Joe. "That sucker loves to stir in shit and make it stink more. Look at him standing over there with that winter hat pulled down over his motherfucking ears. Why does he wear a felt winter hat in hot weather like this, anyway?"

"Lack of sense," Joe said. "You know he's crazy."

The brothers were getting ready to leave, Tom still searching the crowd for Ashley but aware that his youngest brother had been there long enough to know if Ashley was around.

"They're leaving," Joe said, "and personally I hope Ashley will stay away from here for a while."

"You know Ashley." Bucky said. "He ain't scared of nothing."

After Jasper Jones and the Willis brothers left, the Chicken Shack came back to life and everyone breathed a sigh of relief.

Most people liked Ashley Brooks, and everybody in the place knew about the fight between Ashley and Tank, as well as the trouble his father was in. They understood that both Ashley and Stoner had done what they had to do, but nonetheless they were afraid of what the outcome might be.

By now it was almost unbearably hot inside the Chicken Shack. Every face there was showing strain from the heat, but it hadn't stopped the dancing and the good-timing.

Bucky wiped his forehead and his neck with his handkerchief. Tick was sweating profusely too but didn't take out his handkerchief because he was too busy looking for Ruth; he had been watching the door constantly since they'd been there, hoping to see her come in any minute.

"Man, let's get out of this place before I bake!" Bucky said to Tick.

Ella Mae Johnson noticed Bucky and Tick moving toward the door, and she rushed outside ahead of them, hoping to get attention from Tick, whom she had loved since grade school. Back then he would

catch her in the hall coming from the restroom and
feel on her until she reached the door of Mrs. Mills's
third-grade class. If no one else was in the hall she
would stand there for a few seconds and let Tick have
his way with his quick hands while she softly moaned,
"Stop, stop now, stop."

Outside the Chicken Shack, Ella Mae noticed
Bucky's old Ford parked by the pump; she was sure
that Tick had come with Bucky. She hurried toward
the car. Now was the opportune time to get that handsome, skinny devil for the rest of the evening, all to
herself, she thought. She was glad Ruth hadn't shown
up.

Bucky was all right but he thought he was better
than anybody else—too good for her—but that was
all right. Tick was a good kisser and didn't waste time
getting right down to what she wanted from him—
and all she wanted was to get Tick in the backseat of
Bucky's car. It might take some doing; he had changed
a lot since he started pursuing Ruth.

Ella Mae stood against Bucky's car with both arms
folded under her bosom, waiting, occasionally drawing hard on the cigarette she held between her fingers,
throwing her head back and blowing the smoke slowly into the air. The purple silk dress she wore clung
to her oversized hips, making them look like two bas-
ketballs undercover. Only the very tips of her large
bust were covered by the dress that adhered to her
body. Her spiked heels dug deep into the white, sandy
earth, from the tremendous weight of her body. And
her blood-red lips, like the rest of her round face, were
overpainted. When she smiled, she tried to keep her

smiles quick and short, to avoid exposing the gap between her front teeth, big enough to stick a pencil through.

She was chewing hard and fast on gum when she spotted Tick and Bucky coming. She looked in another direction, took a big drag of her cigarette, held her head back, and slowly exhaled. She didn't want Tick to know that she was waiting for him; she was simply resting against the car, taking a smoke.

Tick spotted her. He jabbed Bucky with an elbow. "Look, look, look," he whispered. "There's old Ella Mae. Wants me to do it to her again."

Bucky laughed. "She wants everybody to do it to her, but I think she likes your dick better."

Ella Mae looked around and smiled when Tick and Bucky approached the car. Tick walked up to her and put his arm around her waist. She stopped chewing and grinned, exposing her large gap. "Thought maybe y'all would give me a ride home," she said. Bucky glanced Tick's way and tried to keep from laughing at Ella Mae's sham. Tick winked at him.

She climbed into the back of Bucky's car and Tick crawled in after her, but he glanced back to see if Ruth might have come up at the last minute.

As Bucky drove along slowly he could smell Ella Mae's sweet perfume permeating the inside of his car. He smiled, listening to her occasional sighs and moans coming from under Tick's body.

Chapter 3

It was a sticky, hot night and Ashley was lying across his bed staring at the ceiling, unable to get to sleep. There was too much on his mind. He hadn't felt like going down to the Chicken Shack; it wouldn't have been any fun holding a girl in his arms while his mind was someplace else, and he couldn't seem to get his mind on anything but his father's coming trial.

What if they sent Stoner to jail? Would his family, his mother especially, be able to endure something like that? Ashley had never seen a stronger bond between two people than there was between his parents. They had married when they were teenagers, had come to live on the Brinkley farm, and had to make do with what little the crops brought each year. Despite the hard times their love for each other had grown stronger through the years. His father was one of the proudest men in Mason County, proud of his family and proud of his health and strength and his ability to farm the land and take care of his wife and children.

Ashley didn't know if he could stand visiting his father in prison and watching him slowly shrivel up and die. While Stoner was dying in prison, his mother would be.... Ashley stopped himself; he couldn't allow himself even to think what would happen to his mother.

It couldn't happen—they just couldn't throw his father in jail; Ashley would hold onto that thought to keep from worrying himself sick.

Ashley tossed and turned in the stifling air of his room for a few more minutes and then got out of bed and tiptoed out of the house to the porch, where he sat down on the top step. Outside there was a cool breeze blowing, and he threw back his head and drank it in. His eyes stopped at the sight of the still, peaceful sky, which reminded him of his grandmother. He sat with his head back for a few minutes, studying that awesome wonder over his head.

"Grandma," he whispered, "if they put daddy in jail it will simply tear mama's heart right out of her body."

On Saturday morning Ashley had to take a load of stove wood to Mr. Jenkins's wood yard in town for Mr. Peterson. Ashley had told Minnie and Eva that he might let them ride into town with him. Minnie had begged him to go, and he had said he would think about it. He had been reluctant to say yes. He had heard about the dangers to pretty girls when some city slicker happened to come through town, flashing a gold tooth and a wad of money.

Minnie and Eva were Ashley's younger sisters. Minnie was fourteen and favored her father. Eva was seven and looked a lot like her mother.

Minnie never got to go anywhere. She worked hard at home like a little woman. Everyone said she and Ashley could go for twins.

Ashley adored the way boys were drawn to her, and Minnie loved every minute of it.

It was Ashley who escorted Minnie any place she went out of the watchful eyes of her parents, and when he did take her he was careful not to let her out of his sight.

Minnie had their parents' permission to go to town with him that day, but the final decision was Ashley's alone. Sometimes when it came to letting his young teenage sister go places, he did not agree with his parents. Times were different from when they were young, he often reminded them.

Minnie hoped and prayed that Ashley would decide to let her and Eva go with him to town this morning. She had her fingers crossed, not to mention her toes and her eyes and anything else she could cross.

Just about all the girls at school had seen the scary picture show at the schoolhouse on Saturday. But it wasn't just the movie itself she wanted to see. She hoped she would see Buddyboy Hall at the picture show, even though she knew he couldn't sit with her. She had gotten the message that day in town when Ashley had returned to the truck to find Buddyboy standing there talking to her through the truck window. Ashley hadn't said anything to her or Buddyboy, but his frown had told them everything.

Still, Buddyboy was the handsomest boy at school, and all the girls were dying for him to as much as talk to them, and he liked talking to *her*. Just seeing him and talking to him was enough of a thrill for Minnie—*if* Buddyboy came to the show, and *if* Ashley let her go.

Minnie knew how Ashley was. She realized he wouldn't let her out of his sight the minute they got to town, unless she was sitting alone with Eva protected in the little movie house where everybody knew them.

Early that morning, after Ashley had left for Mr. Peterson's to pick up the truckload of wood, Minnie had worked extra hard at her chores, in the hopes of impressing Ashley, when he stopped by to change clothes and get breakfast, into seeing that she deserved a trip to town. She had thoroughly ironed and creased Ashley's blue jeans, making a crease sharp enough to cut; she had spit-shined his Sunday shoes; and she had cleaned his room so well that he would wonder if he was in the wrong house.

Bessie hadn't felt well this morning, so Minnie had combed and plaited Eva's hair and gotten her dressed to look as nice as possible in town—in case Ashley let them go.

Then, with everything done, they had gone outside to wait for Ashley to come back from Mr. Peterson's. Of course, that meant Minnie had to keep a sharp eye on Eva to keep her looking clean and neat.

"Stop playing in that mud, Eva, before you get your

dress dirty!" Minnie yelled to her sister, as she stood on the front porch and saw that Eva was about to plunge her hands into a mudhole to make a mudcake.

Eva turned and started to stick out her tongue at Minnie, then thought better of it and obeyed her sister. She too wanted to do everything possible to persuade Ashley to let them go to town and see the picture show and eat hot dogs and ice cream.

Minnie dreaded the possibility that Ashley might say no. As she sat on the swing beside the brown bag containing Ashley's breakfast, she anxiously leaned over and secured the fold at the top of the bag. She had been in a happy frame of mind when she had packed the food, humming a song she had learned at school. She had made certain that Ashley's biscuits were filled fuller than hers and Eva's. For him, she had selected the biggest, brownest biscuits, hot from the oven, and sliced them open, filling some with fried side meat and the rest with blackberry preserves.

Minnie walked to the edge of the porch and listened. Her heart began pounding hard when she heard the pickup coming down the path. She ran and got the bag from the chair and braced herself for what Ashley would say.

By the time he headed home to change clothes and get something for breakfast, Ashley had still not decided whether to take Minnie and Eva along with him to town.

The weather-beaten Brooks home stood out in the middle of an open field. A long, white sandy path, with fields of green waving corn on either side in summer, stretched from the main road up to the house.

Driving up the path, as Ashley approached the house, the first thing that popped into view was the well in the front yard, then the house, a rusty gray, which was supported all around with pillars of large rocks. On the front porch, high up off the ground, was a homemade wooden swing at the left end. A grassless yard surrounded the house. Minnie kept the yard immaculately clean with a brush broom, the same kind of broom, made of tree branches tied together, that the country folk had used to sweep their yards for generations.

Always, after Minnie had finished brushing the yard, the broom left a pattern on the white sandy ground that made it look as though the house was surrounded by white carpet.

Under the front porch, Stoner kept white potatoes spread out on the ground, and each morning Bessie bent down under the porch to collect some in a basin to prepare for dinner.

When Ashley saw his two sisters waiting for him in front of the house, he made his decision. The look of hopeful expectation on their faces melted his heart, and he could not bear to disappoint them.

Ashley pulled the truck up by the well, stopped, and jumped out. Eva, grinning, ran up to meet him. He scoured a hand over the top of her head and they walked toward the porch, his hand resting on her head affectionately.

Minnie stood motionless on the porch, grasping a brown bag that Ashley knew contained breakfast food. Her eyes gazed at Ashley as he and Eva walked up to her.

A smile played at the corner of Ashley's lips and he held Minnie's gaze. "Y'all can go," he said, and Minnie and Eva jumped for joy, hugging each other and thanking Ashley.

Ashley went inside to clean up and to change into a white T-shirt and jeans, making sure that his curly hair was neatly combed. Then he went back out to the front porch, where Minnie and Eva were waiting anxiously to leave.

Bessie stood in the front door talking to them. "What time will y'all be back?" she asked Ashley, who stood with his arms akimbo at the edge of the porch, about to walk down the steps.

"Before dark," Ashley said.

Bessie walked out on the porch and examined Minnie and Eva from head to toe to make certain they looked their best. Eva's two back plaits of hair were sticking out and she smoothed them down straight. Both girls wore freshly ironed cotton dresses, Minnie's blue-flowered and Eva's yellow-flowered. Bessie tucked the facing of Minnie's dress into place across her shoulders and pulled her single plait of hair straight down behind her back.

Ashley stood watching Bessie, who had a dour expression on her face, with her lips pressed firmly together. He thought she looked tired. He wished the trial was over and done with so his family could breathe freely. Minnie and Eva said good-bye to Bessie and raced down the steps and out to the truck, scattering the chickens that were pecking and scratching out by the well.

Ashley turned to Bessie. "We'll see you this evening, Ma," he said.

"Be careful, son."

Ashley walked down the steps and toward the pickup truck, taking long strides and whistling. When he reached the truck Minnie and Eva were fighting about who would sit next to the window. Just as Ashley started the truck he looked around and saw Bessie running down the steps of the porch.

"Don't forget, Ashley," she yelled, a hand cupped to the side of her lips, "a half a pound of cheese and a pound of weiners, and a spool of white thread."

It was only eight o'clock. And as Ashley sped down the main highway, cool morning air rushed through the open windows. He relaxed in the seat and laid his arm across the window, his elbow jutting out. He began to whistle softly, staring straight ahead at the gray highway unraveling.

Minnie and Eva sat quiet as mice, watching the green wilderness flying past them, for there was nothing else in sight on the long highway this early in the morning except an occasional mule and wagon with a load of tobacco or hay, the mule plopping along slowly. Ashley would wave at the driver when he pulled around the wagon, because he knew practically everybody in Mason County.

Minnie and Eva were on their best behavior, not wanting to do anything that might possibly hurt their chances of coming with Ashley again. Eva sat trying to adjust her feet on the hump, sandwiched between Ashley and Minnie, having lost out in the competition for the window. Minnie sat watching Ashley out of the corner of her eye, aware that something was bothering him, something other than the trouble their father was in. She unfolded the brown paper sack, reached her hand down in it, brought up a meat biscuit, and handed it to Ashley.

Ashley looked around and took the biscuit. "Thanks, big girl," he said and bit into the biscuit heartily, for it was the first thing he'd had to eat this morning. He ate that one and a preserves biscuit, and then another meat biscuit, all the while talking and being playful with his sisters. But as soon as he finished eating, he resumed the soft whistling, staring ahead as if his mind was a million miles away.

By the time Ashley pulled the truck into Mr. Jenkins's wood yard the temperature had soared to ninety-eight degrees.

Mr. Jenkins, a short, squat man with large hands, walked up to the truck, wiping sweat from his face and neck with a red-and-white flowered handkerchief. His face was beet-red except for his milky-white forehead under his straw hat. His baggy overalls were open on either side, for it was simply too hot to wear them fastened.

Each time Ashley went there Mr. Jenkins complained about the weather; either it was too *dern* hot or too *dern* cold. Ashley always disagreed with him just for the fun of it, saying he liked it that way.

Today he couldn't help but agree with Mr. Jenkins. "Whew," he said, stepping from the truck, where his back, soaking wet, had been sticking to the leather seat. "Today, you're right, Mr. Jenkins," Ashley said, smiling and shaking his head. "It's just too dern hot."

Jenkins spat tobacco juice across the yard and wiped his mouth with the back of his hand. "Man said we might get a little rain this evening. Corn's drying up."

"Yeah," Ashley said, sweat draining down his temples. "Our garden's dried up. Maybe it'll rain and cool off things." They began to unload the pieces of stove wood neatly stacked on the truck, while making small talk about current events, tobacco harvesting and curing in the barns, when they would take it to the market, how much it might bring this year.

Minnie and Eva found a big shady oak tree, spread an old towel from the truck on the ground beneath it, and they sat waiting patiently for Ashley and Mr. Jenkins to finish unloading the wood.

Ashley occasionally glanced over at his sisters, laughing and talking. Sometimes they had their hands up, their palms slapping together, playing *peas porridge hot*, a hand game children played. There was plenty of time before the little schoolhouse opened up for the movie.

The line in front of the schoolhouse was beginning to grow when Ashley and Minnie and Eva arrived. They got out of the truck and walked up to the man selling tickets. Ashley let go of Eva's hand and bought two tickets, then handed them to a tall, beady-eyed ticket-taker at the door. The man's two gold teeth flashed at Ashley when he smiled and took the tickets. He tore the tickets in half and handed them the stubs.

"Y'all g'on in and sit down now," Ashley said. "I'll be back time the show's over." He watched them disappear down the aisle, with Minnie holding on to Eva as if Eva's life was in jeopardy.

The local folks called the schoolhouse "the Rat Box" because of the big rats that scampered underfoot eating spilled popcorn, but it was one place the bone-tired farmers could go to forget their troubles for a few precious minutes. Sometimes a tired farmer spent the conclusion of the picture with his head dropped, snoring loudly, and with everyone snickering at him.

Ashley glanced one last time down the aisle, then he directed his eyes toward the gold-toothed man, who looked suspicious. Reluctantly he walked away and got in the truck. There was ample time to do what he had to do before the picture show was over. Anyhow, he wouldn't be heading back home until the cool of evening, since the old truck had almost overheated on the way in.

Ashley planned to go by to see Harley Skinner first thing, as he did each time he came to town and had been doing since his first time there with his father when he was fourteen.

Harley Skinner was seventy-one-years-old, the only Negro who owned a business in the town of Mason. He had a general store, which he had inherited from the white man he had worked for most of his life, the man who was actually his father. Aside from being a shrewd businessman, Harley was an avid storyteller, a self-proclaimed prophet, and an expert on Negro history. Because Harley's mother had been the colored housekeeper to his father for years until his father's death, he identified greatly with Booker T.

Washington, whose father had been a white slave-
owner and his mother a colored slave.

Harley was a distinguished-looking man, with a yel-
lowish-white complexion, gray silky hair, and bluish-
brown eyes, which peered at people over wire-rimmed
glasses. Age had bent him considerably, and he tried
to compensate for this by throwing his head high as
he walked, making short, quick steps. The result was
that he looked as if he were an old man trying hard
to walk like a young man.

The first time Ashley had gone to see Harley with
his father, Harley had immediately taken him aside
for an inspirational chat, as he did all young Negroes
who came to his store. "What do you want to be when
you grow up, young man?" Harley had asked bla-
tantly, his eyes narrowed, peering at Ashley over his
glasses.

The question had taken Ashley by surprise. Ashley
stood staring at him with both hands in his pockets,
groping for an answer. At age fourteen, Ashley had
not made up his mind what he wanted to do with his
life.

"Well, let me tell you about a young Negro boy by
the name of Booker T. Washington," Harley said. "He
was a Negro, but he was destined to become one of
the most famous Americans of his time. As a child
he worked in the salt mines of West Virginia." Harley
looked Ashley straight in the eye. "Booker T.
Washington was was born in bondage on April 5,
1856. And like Frederick Douglas, his father had been
a white slave-owner, his mother a colored slave. As
a small boy Booker T. was called one day to the 'big

house' of the Virginia plantation, and there, crowded in among other slaves, he heard his master read them the Emancipation Proclamation and watched the tears stream down his mother's face at the news that they were free.

"After rising at four and working all day in the mines, Booker studied his ABCs with his mother at night by the light of the fire. One day in the dark mines Booker heard the men talking about a Virginia school called Hampton where Negroes were taught trades, and he made up his mind to go there. The people of the town helped him with nickels, dimes, and quarters. When he was fifteen," Harley pointed a finger at Ashley, "about your age, he started out, riding a stagecoach until his money ran out, then walking, working, and begging rides until he reached Hampton. He worked his way through, doing any kind of work to get by.

"Booker was deeply impressed with Samuel C. Armstrong, the founder of Hampton, and by the dedicated New Englanders who taught there. It made him want to become a teacher. After he completed his education, he went home to West Virginia where, to repay those who had helped him save up for his education, he taught children all day and grown-ups at night. Then he was asked to return to Hampton to supervise a special program for sixty Indians coming there to study.

"When Booker was in his mid-twenties, a white banker and a Negro mechanic in an Alabama village wrote to Hampton, asking for a teacher to open a normal school for rural Negroes. General Armstrong sent

Booker. His school was a leaky old church and he was the sole teacher, with an umbrella opened over his desk when it rained. There was a little money for his salary, but none for books, land, or building.

"The young teacher and his students decided to raise funds to build a school. Between sessions in reading, writing, and figuring they laid the foundation and raised the walls. In this way, in 1881, Tuskegee Institute came into being."

After Harley finished his story he looked at Ashley standing wide-eyed in awe and said, "Son you can be anything in this world you want to be." He stepped back, laid a finger on his nose, and studied Ashley for a moment, sizing him up. Then he said, "You look like a lawyer if I ever saw one."

Harley's assessment that day had been Ashley's incentive to strive to finish high school in times when, due to the pressures from parents and from the overseers, the majority of the Negro children dropped out of school before the fifth grade in order to work the fields and harvest the crops.

Before that day Ashley had never even considered the possibility of being anything other than a farm boy for the rest of his natural life; his mother and father and grandmothers and grandfathers before him had been tenant farmers, with no dreams or hopes of being anything else. That day Harley had planted a seed of hope in Ashley, and gradually that seed had materialized into a full-fledged determination to get an education and go to law school.

But now, this particular Saturday morning, while it was early and there probably would be no one in the store except him and Harley, Ashley wanted to avoid Harley's long stories and pep-talks. He wanted to make a deal with Harley.

Bessie's birthday was rapidly approaching, and there was a necklace displayed in Harley's store window that had caught Ashley's eye each time he went there. He could think of nothing else he would rather give Bessie for her birthday.

Lying on a purple velvet cloth in the window, surrounded by watches and rings and stickpins and bracelets, the necklace stood out like nuggets of gold washed up in a pan of sand. It had been in the window for as long as Ashley could remember; bright sun had faded the purple velvet a lavender color. Ashley thought perhaps Harley might be glad to trade up even for the beautiful and handsome knife that Stoner had given him, which he thought the world of.

Ashley ambled down the narrow street in the Negro section of town, where all businesses were owned by white men and run by colored. Ashley pulled the knife from his pocket and stared at it, gently rubbing it with his fingertips; he wanted to make certain it looked as good as he thought—looked good enough for Harley to trade for the necklace. He remembered the day Stoner had given it to him for his sixteenth birthday.

It had been a lean and cold winter. The tobacco and corn hadn't sold well. The meat in the smokehouse was all gone. Bessie's canned goods were down to the jars of squash and tomatoes. The sweet potatoes out in the field, stored in their protective winter house, made of mounds of earth covered with straw and pine needles, were all down to little scraggly things the size of bony fingers. When the crops were all harvested Stoner was left owing "the man" instead of the other way around. He was down to his last dime, except for the money he had saved for a pair of badly needed winter brogans.

When Ashley's birthday came and the family had sat around the kitchen table and enjoyed cake and ice cream, Stoner called Ashley aside, as if what he had to say to him was a secret between just the two of them.

They were standing almost behind the door in Bessie and Stoner's room when Stoner said, his hand behind his back, "Got something for you for your birthday."

Ashley looked at him. "What?" He knew there wasn't a cent except the money Stoner had to buy shoes.

Stoner brought forth a beautiful knife and held it in the palm of his hand. Ashley stared at it, his mouth hanging open. It was long and sleek and curved at one end, and the pearly inlay on both sides sparkled like jewels against the silver finish.

"Daddy? Where'd you get that?"

"Go 'head, take it," Stoner said, laying the knife in Ashley's palm. "See what it does." Stoner was so excited that he didn't give Ashley time to examine the knife to discover its features; he jerked the knife back and pulled from its handle a tiny pair of attached scissors, a nail file, a screwdriver, a spoon, a fork. Then he tucked them all back inside the knife handle and stood looking at Ashley with a big grin on his face.

Ashley took the knife back and went through the

same motions, marveling at how odd and beautiful the knife was. He suddenly stopped admiring the knife and looked straight at Stoner.

"Daddy?" Ashley took a long breath. "Did you spend the money for your shoes to...?"

"Don't worry 'bout that. I'll manage," Stoner said.

"But, Daddy? Your shoes?"

"Do you want the knife or not?"

"I love it, Daddy. It's the nicest knife I've ever seen."

"Then put it in your pocket and hush."

Stoner turned and walked away, leaving Ashley standing looking proudly at the knife in his hand. He took it and showed it to the rest of the family. A few days later, just to confirm his suspicions, Ashley took a look inside Stoner's old brogans, which he knew had big holes in the bottoms; sure enough, there were neatly trimmed pieces of cardboard lining the soles.

Ashley slipped the knife back in his pocket as he walked up to Harley's store and pushed open the heavy glass door with the cowbell attached to alert Harley to customers entering.

The old cow bell clanged loudly. Harley, who had been stooping over behind a showcase with only his white hair showing, lifted up as straight as he could and said, "Ashley! It's good to see you, my boy. Thought you'd forgot about old Harley."

"Hey, Mr. Harley. Naw, I ain't never too busy to stop by and holler at you. I ain't been nowhere much lately. Grandma died...and all that." Ashley stood scratching his forehead with his little finger.

Harley's tone of voice was filled with sympathy

when he said, "Yeah, son. I was sorry to hear about your grandmother. Emily Brooks was a fine woman..., fine woman. They don't come any better." He looked up at Ashley. "How's your daddy doing?"

"Daddy's all right, I *guess*," Ashley said. "You heard about the trouble he got in, didn't you?"

"I heard," Harley said, leaning his arms on the top of the showcase. "He'll get out of it. Taylor's the best lawyer anywhere around here.... He'll get out of it."

Ashley took a long breath. "I don't know, Mr. Harley. Ma's scared sick, and I am too. I put up a good front around her, but...I don't know." Ashley was silent for a brief moment, then said, "And Daddy won't even talk about it. Just keeps busy working all the time, looking like he's already been sentenced to life in jail."

Harley asked cheerfully, "What brings you to town this early?"

"Brought a load of wood for Mr. Peterson," Ashley said, slowly moving through the shop, looking at the costume jewelry glittering and sparkling under the bright morning sunshine that streamed in through the windows. "I dropped my sisters off at the picture show," he added, continuing to walk and look. There were many things he could get Bessie for her birthday, but the necklace in the window wouldn't leave his mind. He scratched his scalp through his hair with the tip of his little finger so as not to muss up his hair.

"That necklace you have in the window out there, Mr. Harley," Ashley said, "mind if I see it?"

"Caught your eye, did it?" Harley said, laughing. As if the mention of the necklace had given him added strength, he strode from behind the counter. "Now there's a masterpiece if ever there was one," he said, his eyes sparkling with interest.

Ashley followed him to the window and waited while he got the necklace out. He turned to Ashley, the necklace draped over his palm.

Touching one of the stones gently with his finger-tip Ashley said, "Boy, that's a pretty thing!"

Harley led him back to the counter where he had been standing and pulled out a black velvet cloth, spreading it out and placing the necklace on it as if it were around someone's neck.

"This ain't no ordinary necklace, son," Harley said, as the necklace lay shimmering now like fire. "There's a long story behind this necklace." He pulled up a stool and sat on it, inviting Ashley to pull up a stool as well.

The necklace was one single strand of diamonds, with a single teardrop diamond in the center. And the longer Ashley glared at it shooting out red and green and blue and yellow sparks, the more he realized how valuable it must be.

"Are those real diamonds?" he asked, looking up at Harley, a quizzical frown on his forehead.

"The best," Harley said.

"Wow!" Ashley said. "I didn't realize...."

"Looks the same as it looked on Miss Nellie's neck the day they buried her," Harley said, lifting a bushy gray eyebrow to glance up at Ashley, anxious to get on with the story.

Ashley's eyes shot to Harley's face. "What'd you say?"

"I said it looks the same as it looked on Miss Nellie Flowers's neck the day they buried her."

Ashley grinned at Harley in disbelief. "You mean somebody was buried in that necklace?"

"Exactly," Harley said. "Miss Nellie Flowers. This necklace once belonged to her." And Harley began his story.

"Miss Nellie lived up in the field behind Mr. Lamb's house; Mr. Lamb was our bossman. O-o-o-ld, she was. Nobody knew just how old she was, but everybody speculated she was over a hundred when she died. Looked like walking death, eyes sunk back in her head, skin sagging from her bones like curtains hanging from a rod.

"First time I saw Miss Nellie was the day Mr. Lamb sent me over there with Mammie—I called my mother Mammie. He sent me over there to cut Miss Nellie some firewood, because she didn't have any living relatives except two grown nephews who had visited her only twice in their lives. The first time was to search the house for the necklace and the second time was to sneak to the funeral to see if they were burying the necklace on her.

"See, Mammie used to go over to Miss Nellie's house every day to take her a hot dinner left over from our dinner, and to clean up the house and bathe Miss Nelly."

The curiosity was killing Ashley. "How did that necklace get off Miss Nellie's neck?"

"I'm coming to that. As I said, Mammie and I used to go over to Miss Nellie's house every evening." Harley looked up at Ashley. "See, Mammie and I lived in Mr. Lamb's house. Mammie kept house and cooked for him before I was born.

"Anyhow, one day while Mammie was bathing Miss Nellie she came across this little dingy tobacco sack pinned to Miss Nellie's slip. It was then that Miss Nellie told Mammie all about the diamond necklace she inherited from her grandmother. She had been hiding it on her person ever since the two nephews visited her, one keeping her engrossed in conversation while the other tore the house to pieces looking for the necklace.

"About a week before Miss Nellie died she called Mammie to her and told her she wanted *her* to have the necklace. Well, Mammie knew how much that necklace meant to Miss Nellie. She thanked her and took the necklace, but she had no intentions of keeping it. And the day Miss Nellie died, a few minutes before they lowered her casket into the ground, Mammie opened the casket lid and slipped the necklace around Miss Nellie's neck. The last thing I saw was this necklace around Miss Nellie's throat glittering like fire.

"There wasn't but six people at Miss Nellie's funeral—Mammie, Mr. Lamb, the preacher, and myself, and two strange men who said they were just passing through and wanted to pay their respects. They turned out to be the two nephews.

"Then one cold wintry night, old Jake, a colored man who lived up in the woods not too far from us, was hunting bobcat and spotted a light over in the cemetery."

Harley suddenly got tickled and couldn't continue

for laughing. He bent double, slapping his thigh, and Ashley began to laugh, too. Harley continued, tears in his eyes. "Old Jake tore his breeches running through the woods, thinking it was Miss Nellie's ghost after him. Later on Jake told Mr. Lamb about the light he'd seen, and because Mr. Lamb knew all about the expensive necklace and suspected something strange had taken place, he called out Sheriff Wendy to the gravesite and they found out that Miss Nellie's coffin had been dug up and the necklace taken."

Harley stared down at the floor for a few seconds, as if in deep thought. "That Sheriff Wendy is a son of a bitch when it comes to getting his man," he said. He looked at Ashley with narrowed eyes. "And talk about prejudiced!" Harley whistled. "Hates the fat on a nigger's gut. Well, anyhow, the authorities all told Mr. Lamb that since Miss Nellie gave Mammie the necklace it was rightly hers. Mammie kept that necklace and cherished it till the day before she died, when she called me to her bedside and placed it in my hand." Harley looked down at the necklace. "Ain't she a beauty?" He left to put the necklace back in the window and when he came back, his head thrown high, making little quick, short steps, he stopped and winked at Ashley, saying, "The day a man with enough money comes in here and wants to buy that necklace is the day old Harley will retire."

Ashley smiled, glad that he hadn't mentioned trading his knife for the necklace. Anyway, as soon as he had discovered that the diamonds were real, he had decided on a silver bracelet for Bessie.

Chapter 4

Ashley had parked the pickup under a big shady oak. He stood leaning against the truck fender licking a double scoop of strawberry ice cream, and Minnie and Eva, sitting in the truck with both doors swung open, sat licking their double-scoop cones.

"Eva, you're not licking fast enough," Minnie said to her little sister, who had pink dribbles of ice cream running along the back of her hand and on down to her elbow. Minnie had been disappointed that Buddyboy Hall had not been at the picture show, and she had been watching out the truck window with bated breath, hoping to spot him amongst the people milling along the sidewalk across the street. She reached over and snatched Eva's ice cream cone from her and began licking it rapidly to clean off the melting ice cream.

Eva reached over and snatched it back, "Gimme my ice cream!" she said, a pink mustache on her upper lip.

"Well, stop licking so slow then," Minnie said, looking around for something to wipe her sister's face and hands.

Ashley straightened, pulled out his handkerchief, and walked up to Eva to wipe her face and fingers and arm, then poked the sticky handkerchief back in his pocket, all the while gripping the last of his ice cream between his teeth.

It was around twelve noon, and there had been time for people to get to town, women and young girls walking along in brightly colored cotton dresses, their hips swaying freely underneath, some short, some tall, some jet black, and some lemony yellow or high brown, all walking along the streets and sidewalks with their heads held high as if, now that their feet had touched down on the streets of town, all of their cares had been left at home along with the work-clothes and for now life held only merriment and glee.

And men, young and old, some in clean work clothes because they had to rush back to the fields to finish some urgent task, and others dressed in their usual Saturday attire, all strolled along with their Saturday spirits soaring.

Ashley leaned against the truck, watching the people walk by. There was something that was almost narcotic about standing with the cool breezes gently nudging your face and watching good-hearted fellow-men stroll along. But there still was that little uneasy feeling in his gut, like being awakened at night by the buzz of a mosquito at his ear.

Ashley heard someone calling him from across the street. When he looked, he saw Tick standing in front of Slim's Cafe motioning him over, his body so tall and slender that he looked like a pencil wearing clothes.

Ashley didn't rush. Before responding to Tick, he walked up to the truck cab, looked over at Minnie, and said, "Y'all stay here till I come back. I'll bring you back a hot dog and a drink." Then he trotted across the street to where Tick stood waiting. He knew exactly what Tick wanted to talk about and he didn't feel like getting into all that business about Tom and Lewis Willis being after him. But he wasn't running either.

"Get your tail over here!" Tick said with a tone of urgency, in his voice. Ashley approached Tick, smoothing his hair back and wiping his mouth to make certain he was rid of all the ice cream.

"Where you been, man?" Tick said, frowning, cupping a hand over his eyes to ward off the blinding noon sun. "You better stay away from them Willis boys. Come on. Let's go in here where Bucky is." And he turned toward Slim's Cafe. The two of them, side by side, taking long strides, Tick's longer than Ashley's, walked toward the cafe.

When they entered Slim's the loud jukebox music and the tantalizing aromas of onions and chili hit them head-on. The popular Saturday gathering place was beginning to crowd up, some people sitting, laughing, talking, eating, and drinking on the stools along the front of the long counter almost the length of the cafe, and others sitting in shadowy booths with little tables and red leather upholstered seats. It was dark and cool inside, a big fan whirring lazily in the ceiling.

Ashley followed Tick over to where Bucky sat at the counter, straddling a stool and leaning toward the counter as he finished a hot dog. Tick climbed on a stool, leaving one for Ashley between him and Bucky.

Ashley sat on the stool in a slow, unperturbed manner, and Bucky, looking around at him, said, "Hey, man. We been looking for you. I'm glad you wasn't crazy enough to come to the Chicken Shack Saturday night. Them Willis boys was there just itching to get their hands on you."

Ashley stared at Bucky from the corner of his eye. "I didn't feel like going nowhere. I had a lot on my mind. I stayed home and went to bed early." Ashley wanted to make it clear that it wasn't because he was scared that he hadn't gone to the Chicken Shack, even if the fact that he didn't go might have been because he didn't want to make trouble with the Willis boys.

"It's a good thing you did," Tick said, finishing off the barbecue sandwich he had left half-eaten when he had spotted Ashley and jumped up to go call him. "They came by the Chicken Shack just long enough to peep in and see if you was there. Then they got the hell out of there like they was going to find you," Tick said, a worried-looking glint in his eyes.

"That Tom Willis is crazy," Bucky said. "Either you have to kill him or stay away from him. I don't want to see you get in trouble, man, but if you just say the word I'll help you catch Tom Willis off guard, when he ain't got that old shotgun handy, and beat the hell out of him."

Ashley sat silently for a brief second, staring thoughtfully at the ashtray on the counter. Then he got up and walked to the window, looking out across the street to where the pickup was parked. Minnie and Eva were still sitting in the truck as he had left them. Ashley stood there a minute longer, looking up and down the street, then he walked back and sat on the stool.

Unbeknownst to Ashley, a pair of eyes had been watching him since he first entered the cafe. The eyes belonged to Daisy Lane, the attractive waitress behind the counter. She pretended—or tried to pretend—that Ashley was just another customer, but truth was that she loved him so much that it was almost unbearable. She could still remember the night they had actually touched. It was at the Chicken Shack when he'd asked her to dance, not knowing that she had inched her way across the entire length of the floor just as the slow record came on the jukebox, hoping Ashley would choose her to dance with over the five other girls standing waiting with bated breaths.

The few times that Daisy's mother had allowed her to go to the Chicken Shack were precious to her; they had been her big chances to see Ashley. But she wanted to see more of him. And that had been one of the reasons she had gone through hell and high water to persuade her father to let her take the waitress job at Slim's Cafe, so she would be able to see Ashley more often.

Out of the corner of her eye, Daisy had noticed the way Ashley's white T-shirt hugged every muscle in his upper body. And that slow-and-steady-but-sure gait of his sent chills up her spine.

Ashley had looked up and smiled and said hello just after he had walked in and straddled the stool. Daisy knew it was only because he remembered dancing with her that night, and nothing more. She walked about waiting on customers, and between customers she wiped the counter repeatedly, while Ashley and Tick and Bucky talked quietly among themselves.

Ashley stuck his finger in the air and beckoned Daisy over to him. After ordering two hot dogs and a grape drink, he sat eating heartily and laughing and talking and joking with Bucky and Tick. Daisy watched him out of the corner of her eye, noting each movement of his mouth as he chewed, his strong jaw-line, the lean shoulders.

When Ashley finished eating he beckoned her over again and this time ordered hot dogs and bottled drinks to go. He walked out carrying them oh-so-carefully in his hands.

Daisy's heart sank. She thought he was gone for good; she wanted him to stay forever. Then he came back and sat down again. She eased to the window and looked out to see who he had taken the food to. She saw two heads in the green pickup and knew they were his two sisters. She was deeply relieved.

Daisy could still feel the electrical shock that had surged through her when she had handed Ashley his change and their fingers had touched for a brief moment. She could feel his arms around her the way they had felt the night he held her when they danced at the Chicken Shack. She looked over and saw him standing to leave. She felt sad enough to cry.

"I'm going on," Ashley said, standing and stretching. "Minnie and Eva must be tired of waiting. I got to take care of some more business. Maybe by that time it'll be cool enough to head on back home. The truck almost overheated on me coming down here."

"Yeah," Tick said, looking up at Ashley. "If I was you I'd keep a close watch on your sisters. Ain't no telling what Tom Willis will do to get even with you."

Ashley looked straight at him but didn't respond. "I'll see y'all," he said and walked out.

Ashley had gone by the Brinkley warehouse and picked up a hoe handle and a new harness for the dapple-gray mule he used for plowing. He had taken care of unfinished business at Tony's funeral home concerning his grandmother's recent death, and he had picked up the things Bessie had asked for.

It was around six o'clock now and the weather had cooled off considerably. He was on his way home, driving the pickup down Beacon street—deliberately taking Beacon because that was where the court house was. It was coming into view, its red-brick facade somber and intimidating. Taking a good look at it would help ease the tension. It loomed larger and larger as he drove toward it. He thought of the blind justice that lay behind those stately walls—more than blind for Negroes, who were already assumed guilty when they entered the door.

Ashley had read about the case of the nine Scottsboro boys a few years before. Nine Negro boys were hoboing around the country on a freight in search of work. At Scottsboro, Alabama, they were hauled off the train by police, who also found two white women hoboes in a coal car. The police promptly accused the nine black boys of rape. One boy was only thirteen. A hasty trial was held before an all-white jury, which quickly convicted the other eight boys and they were sent to the "death house" at Kilby. Defended by the Communist International Labor Defense, the Scottsboro Case became a *cause celebre*, fought all the way to the Supreme Court. None of the boys were executed, but all served long years in prison. This case aroused worldwide protest and pointed up the inequities of southern courts and the lily-white system.

Ashley was aware that some Negroes were not even that lucky.

He drove on out of town and hit the main highway. Cool, damp air, mixed with the odor of corn, tall and green and gently swaying in the evening breeze, beat against their faces through the open windows. Ashley sat very quietly, thinking, staring down the road, and Minnie and Eva sat quietly because he was quiet, Minnie occasionally glancing over at him to make sure he wasn't falling asleep.

Even though Ashley was quiet on the outside, his mind was filled with voices shouting back and forth about him and his future.

Yes, he can. He can do it. Look what other Negroes, like Booker T. Washington, have done.

No, he can't. How will he ever become a lawyer with the meager education he got at that three-room school? He won't be able to compete with students in college who attended good city schools. And besides, he needs to stay home and take his daddy's place because his daddy will be in jail.

Ashley began to whistle to drown out the voices. Then he was suddenly aware of his sisters. He glanced at them, reaching over and tweaking Eva's nose, then reaching behind Eva's head and yanking Minnie's plait of hair.

They felt much better. Seeing Ashley sad had made them sad.

Chapter 5

Rosa Mae Eatman was Bessie Brooks's sister and she looked like Bessie, but she was two years older. The morning Ashley had gone into his grandmother's room and found her dying, he had run down the long dusty road to his Aunt Rosa's house for help.

Rosa was standing in her kitchen now, looking into the small mirror on the wall. She was married to an abusive husband, and Leonard had busted her lip. It was swollen and already turning purple. For years she had been promising herself that she was going to leave him.

"Thinks he can hit me when he gets ready!" Rosa said, sniffling. "One of these days he'll look up and I won't be here!"

With that consoling thought, Rosa stopped crying and wiped her face with the end of her apron. She washed the breakfast dishes, trying not to cry, but the tears kept falling, hot and salty, running in her mouth.

Twenty years ago when she had married Leonard he had been sweet and gentle. But within the past few years he had become almost impossible to live with, due to his jealous rages, accusing her of being with other men behind his back.

Yesterday she had walked up the road to Bessie's house. They had sat talking most of the time about Stoner and the trouble he was in. Rosa left Bessie's a little before sunset and on her way back down the road she stopped at Addie Turl's house. Addie had been ill and was just getting back on her feet, and Rosa had wanted to see if there was anything she could do for her.

Leonard was jealous of Addie's husband, Luke. When Rosa got home around dusk, Leonard was waiting for her in the yard. She told him the truth, that she had stopped by Addie's house, but before she could tell him that Luke hadn't been there, Leonard's fist had smashed against her face, sending her staggering across the yard. Then as she stood with her hand cupped over her bleeding lip, he kept making advances toward her to hit her again, refusing to believe anything but that she had been in the cornfield with Luke.

That night she had cried herself to sleep on the very edge of her side of the bed, while Leonard slept on his side like a baby. This morning she had risen at dawn, as usual, and prepared Leonard's breakfast. He had come into the kitchen, sat down at the table, and chewed and smacked and eaten, and then had gone to work, without saying a single word. And Rosa had said nothing to him.

Rosa didn't know how much more she could take of Leonard's uncontrollable anger, or of the embarrassment she felt each time she had run up to Bessie's house begging Bessie to hide her, while the children looking on wide-eyed. Rosa suspected that one day Ashley was going to hurt Leonard if this kept up. She had noticed the angry glint in Ashley's eyes and the way his jaws twitched when Ashley had come to the door this time, then stood looking down the road as if daring Leonard to try to come up there.

Rosa finished the dishes, got a chair, and went out to sit under the shade of the pecan tree in the front yard. It was as quiet as the grave, except for the hum of flies and an occasional bark of a dog far, far away. She looked up at the sky, bright blue with little white clouds floating lazily along. The loneliness she felt was enough to make her cry.

Mr. Peterson had bought a new truck, and he had insisted that Ashley keep the old green pickup at his house to drive back and forth to work, and to use for his own personal needs.

Ashley had promised George Brown that he would come by and pick him up, since the man George usually rode with was sick. George was a good friend of the Brooks family, and he worked with Ashley on Peterson's farm. But Ashley was reluctant about going to George's house, because George's young wife, Bumpsy, had more than once openly displayed her attraction to him, and he was afraid that sooner or later George was going to catch her.

Ashley slowed the truck down, turned off the highway, and followed the narrow path through a grove of trees. When he came out of the grove he could see George's house; Bumpsy was at the well, drawing water. She was wearing a pair of red pants that had been snipped off at the bottom—snipped off so short that it looked as though she was wearing a pair of red underwear with red fringe around the bottom.

The first time Ashley had seen Bumpsy was the night Bucky and Tick had thrown a wild party at Bucky's house. This wasn't long after Bumpsy's grandmother had died, and the seventeen-year-old girl, who had been living with her grandmother, was being passed back and forth from one relative to the other like a hot sweet potato. None wanted the responsibility of a young, promiscuous girl like Bumpsy.

It was a hot summer night and the moon was shining down on the guests at the party. It was the only light in the yard except for the faint glow of a lamp coming from the window of Bucky's house, where he lived alone.

Bucky had the phonograph sitting on the well shelf with the volume turned up to the last notch, and there were several gallons of grape punch, as well as plates of assorted cookies, on a long table in the middle of the yard, the white sheet serving as a tablecloth waving in the moonlight. Tick had sneaked up to the tub of punch and emptied a jar of white lightning into it.

Back at her house, Ashley's girl at the time, Iva Jean Jones, had jumped out of the truck and slammed

the door and said it was over between them because
Ashley kept insisting he wasn't ready to get married,
that he wanted to go to college. Ashley had left her
house and come straight to the party.

When he drove up, all he could see before the headlights was swirling dust being kicked up by dancing
couples at the party in Bucky's grassless front yard.
Ashley noticed several couples walking down the path
toward the cornfield, and some coming out of the
cornfield.

Tick had been waiting for Ashley, and he came up
to the truck as soon as he arrived. "Where's Iva Jean?"
he asked Ashley.

Ashley slid off the seat to the ground and slammed
the truck door shut before he answered. "Who's worried about Iva Jean? I came here to have a good time.
Where's the girls?"

Tick looked at Ashley through the darkness. "Well,
in that case, I got one for you. You ever heard of
Bumpsy Jones?"

"Yeah," Ashley said.

Tick leaned over to Ashley's ear and whispered,
"I'd like to get her behind the house myself, but Ruth's
here." Ashley could smell the alcohol on Tick's
breath. "There she is over there, sitting on the
doorstep," Tick said. "Come on." Ashley followed
him. Tick introduced them and left.

"Are you crying?" Ashley asked Bumpsy, bending
to look in her face because she was sitting with her
head lowered and wiping her eyes. She didn't answer.
"You're supposed to be having a good time," Ashley
continued. "Why the tears?"

Bumpsy was silent for a second; then in a low tone of voice she said, "You'd be crying too if you was me."

Ashley eased down on the step beside her. "Now, why would I want to be crying if I was a pretty girl like you?"

"You'd be crying because you didn't have nobody in the whole damn world that cared about you," Bumpsy said, sniffling.

"What happened?" Ashley asked. "Did you just break up with your boyfriend?"

"I don't have a boyfriend or a mother or father or a sister or brother or nobody," Bumpsy said, starting to cry again, and then she told him the whole story of how her grandmother had taken her in when her mother had run away, and how after her grandmother died nobody wanted her. "They don't want me— none of them," she said, wiping her eyes as if she was determined never to cry again.

Ashley looked out in the middle of the yard at the brand-new tin tub full of punch and said, "Want some punch?"

Bumpsy nodded. He walked over to the table and came back with two peanut-butter jars filled with the spiked punch.

Ashley knew at the first sip that the punch had been spiked, and he chuckled to himself, knowing who had done it. He sipped his slowly while Bumpsy drank hers and told him about her hard life, her voice becoming more and more cheerful as her jar became empty.

"Want some more punch?" Ashley asked. He could feel her mellowing under the influence of the raw moonshine. After refilling their jars, he sat down on the top step beside her. She eased up against him. He could feel the softness of her hip pressed close to his.

"I feel better now," Bumpsy said. "I ain't gonna worry no more." She slipped an arm around Ashley. "I got me somebody to like me now." She squeezed him to her and craned her neck to kiss his nose. "You do like me, don't you?"

"Of course I do, baby." Ashley's speech was beginning to slur. He took her in his arms, squeezed her to him, and gently kissed her lips. Five minutes later Bumpsy lay stretched out on the step, her head in Ashley's lap, gazing up at the moon. Ashley worked his hand up to her left breast and squeezed the nipple through her dress, then squeezed the right nipple.

Bumpsy turned over so that her face was close to Ashley's stomach. She slipped up his T-shirt and ran a wet, warm tongue over his navel, using slow, seductive licks. In a flash, Ashley's hand disappeared underneath her dress as he bent over and smothered her with kisses.

"What will your mama and daddy say?" Bumpsy asked, moaning and sighing to the moves of his hand.

"What will my mama and daddy say about what?"

"Say about you taking me home with you?"

"Taking you home with.... Oh, Nothing, baby. Absolutely nothing. I'll take you home with me and hide you under my bed."

Bumpsy sat straight up. "Let's go for a walk," she said. Ashley rose immediately, noticing that now the table in the yard was dancing along with the couples, and that there were two moons. He grabbed Bumpsy's hand and helped her up from the step. Hand in hand they crossed the yard and walked down to the edge of the woods, where they found a spot of spongy grass. They sat upon it and soon they were wallowing all over it, kissing passionately and fondling each other while the seductive music from the Victrola on the well shelf drifted toward them. Then while the frogs croaked loudly and the chorus of the crickets droned on they made passionate love.

By the time they got back to the yard Ashley had sobered. The couples were dancing to a slow record, a blues song by some deep-throated lady singer; the girls were hanging around the necks of their lovers like long necklaces.

Ashley took Bumpsy in his arms and she laced her fingers behind his neck as they fell into slow rhythm with the music, swaying in the cool, damp atmosphere, Ashley's forehead pressed hard against the top of Bumpsy's head.

"You are gonna take me home with you, aren't you?" Bumpsy asked.

Ashley stopped still in his tracks. "Bumpsy, I was just kidding." He laughed. "I couldn't take you home with me unless we were married."

"Then you'll marry me, won't you?" Bumpsy asked, still swaying to the music, her body pressed against Ashley's motionless body.

"Bumpsy…, I didn't mean…. It was the moonshine in the punch."

"Love you, love you, love you," Bumpsy sang along with the record, and it took Ashley thirty minutes to convince her that he couldn't take her home with him.

Bumpsy stood at the well now, looking like a brown Daisy Mae in the *Li'l Abner* comic strip. She was drawing a bucket of water, and it was almost to the top. When she looked up and saw Ashley driving up she didn't bother to pour the water from the well bucket to the kitchen bucket. She quickly fastened the loop of the chain over the nail and left the bucket of water swinging while she rushed out to meet Ashley.

Ashley's father and Bumpsy's husband, George, had been good friends since childhood. After George's wife died, George moped around for years, sad and lonely. Then one of Bumpsy's relatives arranged a meeting for George and Bumpsy. George immediately fell in love with the pretty young girl, cherishing the ground she pranced on. And because Bumpsy desperately needed someone to take care of her, she married George. She had been in love with Ashley ever since the night of Bucky's party. Ashley had a lot of respect for George and stayed clear of Bumpsy, because whenever or wherever she saw him she openly displayed her feelings for him.

Ashley stopped the truck and remained in his seat. As Bumpsy walked over toward him he tried not to notice her shapely thighs in the red shorts and her large breasts jiggling underneath the skimpy blouse.

"Hi, baby! Where you been keeping yourself?"

"Hi, Bumpsy. Is George ready?"

"You sho' is looking good."

"Is George ready?"

"He eating breakfast," Bumpsy said absently, gently rubbing Ashley's arm on the window, looking straight at him, a dreaminess in her eyes.

Ashley thought he had better get out and find George before Bumpsy climbed in the truck with him. He opened the door, slid off the seat, and walked toward the back porch. Bumpsy went back to the well to get the water.

As Ashley stepped up on the rickety porch he could see George hurriedly finishing breakfast, a cup up to his lips, gulping the last of his coffee. His bald head glistened in the sunlight that streamed through the kitchen window.

He saw Ashley and said, "Come on in, Ashley. I'm ready. Just let me get my shirt." And he left the kitchen, his suspenders dangling about his thighs, his old green work pants falling loosely down his wide, flat backside like the skin on an elephant's behind.

Ashley sat down on a twine-bottomed chair next to the kitchen door to wait. Then Bumpsy walked in with the bucket of water, some sloshing on the floor as the screen door slammed behind her.

Ashley immediately stood and took the bucket of water, crossing the kitchen and setting it on the stand next to the washbasin. He turned back and his arm met something soft and spongy; it was Bumpsy's left breast. She had come up behind him and was about to throw her arms around his neck. He stepped backwards, but she followed, hugging and kissing him anyway.

George's heavy footsteps plodding down the hall sent Bumpsy scurrying away from Ashley. Ashley hurried out the back door and was sitting in the truck waiting when George got there. George climbed into the truck and sat down heavily, his bald head studded with beads of sweat. Ashley felt sorry for the old man.

Ashley and George rode along talking about the dry spell that Mason County was suffering, a trail of white dust lingering in the humid atmosphere as far back down the winding dirt road as the eye could see. Ashley's hair fluttered in the wind and George's old blue denim shirtsleeve flapped against his arm as it rested in the window, the old green pickup truck racing along at about thirty-five miles an hour. George said it might rain because his corns ached.

Ashley looked up and saw Iva Jean Jones's house coming into view. He had tried to put her out of his mind since she had gone off to college up North, but something always brought back memories of the good times they had as sweethearts through high school. He still thought she was a wonderful girl. She was attractive, intelligent, determined to make something of herself.

Her father was the only Negro in Mason County who owned land. He saved up his money and bought a piece of bottomland from his bossman. Then with his own two hands he had built a comfortable five-room house with a large front and back porch, enclosing it inside a white picket fence. Mrs. Jones had planted bright red climbing roses alongside the front of the fence, and Mr. Jones had mowed the wild grass each week, giving the place a splendid green lawn.

After the Joneses had bought new furniture for the entire five rooms, including an electric stove for the kitchen, Negroes from miles around had flocked there to marvel that a Negro could own land just like the white man.

Ashley had never been able to make Iva Jean understand why he couldn't marry her—that he had to think of his own education.

With times so hard, it would be difficult enough to go off to college without having the responsibilities of a wife.

Thomas Rucker was fifty-two years old, a tall, brawny man with thin blond hair and icy-blue eyes. He talked out of the side of his mouth.

He was a driven man. Rain or shine he was up and out of the big house before sunup, Monday through Sunday.

He had worked his tail off to be in the position he was in. He had left behind the other poor white cracker boys who were inclined to accept whatever the day brought forth in the nature of things, those whose ambition was so weak that, unless it surged up in their dreams, they never imagined themselves being boss of a plantation.

He cherished his overseeing job, and all he wanted a Negro man to do for him was say "yes, suh" and "no, suh" when he spoke to him. He had an acquired antipathy for Negros, which had been sharpened into hatred. His hatred of blacks—and some poor white farmers—stemmed from jealousy and his own inadequacy in striving to support his family and get ahead.

Rucker's seventeen-year-old blonde, shapely daughter did not share her father's views about Negroes. Mary Jo tugged at the button on her blouse between her voluptuous breasts; it kept popping open from the pressure of what it was meant to conceal. She finally gave up and jerked open her dresser drawer, taking out a strapless little halter and pulling it over her head. If she had her way about it she would wear nothing but shorts—short shorts—and halters to show off her womanly curves to the men.

At first she stepped into a pair of short shorts—hot pink. She quickly pulled them off; she didn't feel like hearing her mother scold her about being half-naked around the black men who came to the big house during the day to get supplies or work in the nearby barns. She selected a pair of shorts that reached almost to her knees. Her mother would approve of these.

Mary Joe hurried to the kitchen. Her mother's eyes immediately washed over her. Mary Jo thought her mother's eyes must surely be as severe as Sheriff Wendy's when he appraised a colored man who was suspected of concealing stolen property.

Alice Rucker said nothing to Mary Jo, though she did not approve of the way her breasts bulged in the skimpy halter; she knew it would do no good to say anything. Instead she dipped the egg-stained dish she had been washing in the hot sudsy water and continued to scrub it, before going on to wash the other dishes waiting in the pan.

Since Sam was no longer doing odd jobs for them, after the dispute over the ham, Mary Jo and Alice had lots to do around the Rucker home. This morning, as soon as Mary Jo finished breakfast, they had to wash windows. Alice had already gotten started on the inside of the kitchen window by the time Mary Jo finished her breakfast and went out to the shed in the backyard to get the ladder she needed to do the outside of the window.

Mary Jo noticed Earl, the twenty-year-old son of a Negro tenant farmer, coming up the path swinging an empty milk pail on his arm. She pretended not to see him and immediately started to struggle with the ladder, knowing Earl would rush to her rescue. With effort, she proceeded to tug the ladder to the side of the house, occasionally sweeping back her long blonde hair with a quick upward flick of her arm behind her head.

Earl quickly dropped his pail to the ground, taking the ladder from her and in no time had it up against the window, directly in the view of Alice, who was standing on the other side, washing the inside of the window.

Mary Jo thanked Earl, a big smile on her face, and while he held the ladder she slithered up it like a lizard up a tree. Earl walked back and picked up his pail and continued to the milk barn to fill it with cold milk.

Alice's eyes burned into those of her daughter through the window. "Really, Mary Jo! Do you have to twist so much before those black boys that pass by?" she said loudly so that Mary Jo could hear her through the closed window.

"Oh, Mother, please. Earl didn't even pay any attention to the way I climbed the ladder."

Alice rolled her eyes at Mary Jo and made a "poot" sound. "Just keep on thinking they don't pay attention to the way you swing your hips and you'll be sorry one day!" Alice finished washing her side of the window in complete silence.

The young colored boy that Mary Joe was more than fond of was Leon Willis. The two of them had met more than once behind the barn to express their mutual feelings for each other. But Leon was no fool. He knew how violent Rucker could get with with a black man for simply talking back to him. Leon was deathly afraid to be seen admiring Mary Jo's lovely body from afar, not to mention holding that gorgeous body in his arms and smothering her with kisses.

Leon knew of the trouble Stoner Brooks was in with Rucker, and he could imagine a nigger-hater like Rucker sitting on the witness stand lying through his teeth.

Leon Willis was the eighteen-year-old first cousin of the three Willis brothers, but he would just as soon disown them. Leon lived and breathed for the times when he could see Mary Jo.

Chapter 6

It was Ashley's birthday, and it was certain that Bessie would have the big mixing bowl down from the top of the pie safe and, using the big brown eggs she had saved up, she would be mixing up a cake for him before the sun was all the way up.

When Ashley walked into the kitchen that morning he decided it was the opportune moment to have a heart-to-heart talk with her about the upcoming trial. Things had been too quiet, only the stress showing in their faces. It needed talking about. Stoner refused to even mention it, and all Bessie would say was, "Son, don't worry. Your daddy's a good man. God will see him through this."

Stoner had driven the mule and wagon into town for supplies from the Brinkley warehouse, at Mr. Brinkley's request. Mr. Brinkley warned him not to go near Thomas Rucker. He also told Stoner that, no matter what the outcome of the trial, he should consider moving his family to another farm. "You and Thomas Rucker will never be able to get along after what's happened."

But Stoner had already been offered the five-room house on Mr. Peterson's farm. Peterson had built the house for his oldest son and his family. They had lived in the house one year before deciding to move to town. Stoner could move his family in the first of the year and work for Peterson from then on.

When Ashley walked into the kitchen, Bessie's back was to him. She was stirring vigorously in the mixing bowl.

"Where's Daddy?" he asked Bessie.

She turned toward him, relaxing her grip on the old wooden spoon for a moment. "He's already gone to town to get them supplies."

"I told Daddy I'd carry him on the truck. Why didn't he wake me up?"

"You know your daddy as well as I do, Ashley. He wanted you to be able to sleep late this morning since it's your birthday."

"That ain't nothing. I'd 'a' carried him."

Bessie smiled. "It was nice of Mr. Peterson to let you have the day off. He's a good man. Don't find many white men with the kind of heart he's got." She picked up a golden brown egg from a bowl, cracked it open, added it to the cake batter, and began stirring vigorously again.

Ashley crossed the kitchen and pulled open the oven door; from the oven, still warm inside, he removed three large brown biscuits from the biscuit pan and closed the door. Back at the table he filled two with blueberry preserves and one with a big slice of fried shoulder meat. He turned to get coffee, but Bessie had already stopped what she was doing and had the old blue-speckled coffee pot tilted, pouring a mug for him.

Ashley bit heartily into the meat biscuit, chewed vigorously, sipped the coffee, and then said, "Daddy don't look too good lately. That trial is tearing him apart. I can see it all over his face. And he won't talk about it."

Bessie sighed heavily. "It's tearing us all apart. God knows I'll be glad when it's over and your daddy is a free man—and he *is* going to be a free man. I have to believe that."

"If Daddy would just talk about it and not keep it bottled up inside he'd feel better," Ashley said.

"What is there to talk about?" Bessie asked, looking straight at Ashley. "We all know what's happened before in situations like this one. Talking about it only makes it worse. All we can do is hope for the best. By the way, happy birthday."

Ashley knew she was deliberately changing the subject. "Yeah, I'm nineteen," Ashley said. "That only reminds me that I should be entering college this fall, like Iva Jean."

"Iva Jean's father can afford to send her to college," Bessie said. "And don't you go feeling sorry for yourself, son. Your daddy is doing the best he can. You can go to college too. We'll just have to rake and scrape a little harder. We ain't asking you for a penny of that money you're making at Mr. Peterson's. You just keep saving."

Ashley drank the last of the coffee, rubbed his hands together over his plate, and belched. "I need to be doing something toward bettering my education, though, until I can start college," he said, looking thoughtfully out of the window at the big oak down from the house standing motionless except for two top branches moving gently in the morning breeze. He remained silent for a few seconds longer, thinking of that little boy and his mother learning the alphabet by the light of the fire, the boy dead tired from working in the mine all day, yet determined to learn to read.

"I think I'll go by Harley's and get some more books on Negro history," Ashley said. "It makes me feel good to know what our black ancestors accomplished through sheer determination when all the odds were against them."

Bessie looked at him, smiling. "Just listen at him! Using all them big words."

Ashley narrowed his eyes. "Ma, I've got to stop using improper English from habit. I've got to start speaking correctly. I know what's right. It's just a matter of remembering to use the right words. I think I'll see if I can get some books from the school library too. There's..., there are a million things I can do to better my education until I start college."

Ashley got up from the table and scooped a fingerful of Bessie's rich yellow cake batter from the bowl. Bessie slapped his hand.

"On my way to town I think I'll stop by to see how Robert is doing," Ashley said. "If he ain't done..., if he hasn't drunk his fool self to death by now."

Bessie smiled at Ashley correcting himself. "Be back by suppertime, though. I'm fixing a special dinner for your birthday."

Robert Stover was Ashley's best friend. The last time Ashley had seen him he had been on crutches, his leg and wrist in casts; he had fallen from the back of a truck without railings when it had stopped suddenly, breaking his leg and wrist. He was a year older than Ashley, but he looked ten years older. Robert was a heavy drinker.

After the accident, Ashley had told him, "Man, you're gonna kill yourself if you don't stop drinking." But it was a wonder Robert didn't drink more than he did, Ashley thought, since Robert's mother, Hattie, was a bootlegger. It was the way she supported herself and Robert.

On weekends Hattie's house was crowded with farmers who had sweated and toiled in the fields all week and came to her place to find joy and peace in the white, fiery juice she sold. Hattie herself never touched a drop, but her son Robert had fallen under the influence of the stuff.

Hattie's house was not too far from Ashley's house, hidden far back up in the fields behind cottonwood trees. It was impossible to find if one didn't know it was there. Going to Hattie's house on weekends was like going to church; everybody was there. Even friends and relatives who didn't drink gathered there to socialize.

Sheriff Wendy knew about Hattie's livelihood, but for some strange reason he never set foot in her yard; some claimed he said it was because it kept a lot of the niggers off the town square.

When Ashley drove the pickup up to Robert's house he spotted Bumpsy standing at the corner of the house with a man. Bumpsy saw Ashley and darted behind the house. The man hadn't noticed Ashley because his head and eyes were buried in Bumpsy's bosom, his arms around her, squeezing her. Ashley thought about turning around and leaving; he didn't want any rumors getting back to George. But Bumpsy was gone now, so Ashley went on up to the house.

Hattie met Ashley at the door and led him to Robert's room down a hall, which was directly across from two rooms Hattie rented out by the hour.

Robert, tall and skinny, with a front tooth missing, was lying stretched out on the bed on top of a disheveled blue chenille bedspread that had relinquished its vanity to his predicament. His wrist and leg lay motionless on the bed beside him in their plaster of paris molds.

Ashley walked up to the door and stopped. "Ain't that a pitiful shame," he said, shaking his head slowly, teasing Robert.

Robert looked up. "Hey man. Come on in and sit down. I ain't seen you in a coon's age."

Ashley walked in and stopped by the bed. "How you coming along, old buddy?" he asked, his arms akimbo.

"Man, these damn casts is killing the hell out of me. I can't scratch, can't hardly walk, can't do nothing much. How you been?" He was looking up at Ashley, grinning. Ashley laughed.

"Grab a chair, man," Robert said, making himself

as comfortable on the bed as possible.

Ashley sat down in a chair near the door and leaned back against the wall. While he and Robert talked they were interrupted by loud voices coming from one of the rented rooms across the hall.

"You give me my goddamn money, nigger. Ain't nobody in love with you. You paying for this!" a woman shouted.

"Ah, come on, baby," a man's voice said. "Don't be that-a-way." Then something crashed against the wall and the door flew open and someone chased someone down the hall and out the back door.

Ashley looked at Robert and they both laughed. "Old Mattie keeps letting Slick have pussy on credit and he never pays up," Robert said.

Robert maneuvered himself to a sitting position like a robot, his feet on the floor, and reached under the bed to pull out a pint jar one-fourth full of whiskey.

"Want a drink, man?"

Ashley, sitting with his arms up and his fingers laced on top of his head, said, "Naw, man. I can get along just fine without that stuff."

Robert turned the jar up to his lips and took a stiff drink. Frowning, he tightened the lid on the jar and slipped it back under the bed, where it was safely hidden by the sagging bedspread.

"If Ma finds out I'm drinking this stuff she'll beat the hell out of me," Robert said.

Ashley brought his arms down. "Man, how do you expect your bones to heal up drinking that stuff? When are you supposed to go get those things taken off, anyway?"

"In three weeks," Robert said.

"You better hope the doctor takes them off in three weeks," Ashley said. "If you keep drinking and slipping, you gonna be walking around here next year wearing them."

The back screen door slammed and someone chased someone up the hall, into the room across the way, and the door slammed.

Ashley and Robert talked for thirty minutes, then Ashley stretched and said, "Well, I better be getting on. I'm on my way to town. You need anything?"

"Naw, man. I'm being waited on hand and foot. Ma and Bay takes good care of me."

Ashley nodded and grinned. Bay was Robert's girlfriend.

"Bay was over here last night," Robert continued. "She shaved me and gave me a little loving. Said she was gonna marry me soon's I stop drinking." He grinned,

"And when is that gonna be?" Ashley asked, looking straight at Robert, a solemn expression on his face.

"Soon, man. Soon. I swear," Robert said, a serious glint in his eye.

They heard the click of a woman's high heels coming down the hall. Ashley looked around and saw that Bumpsy had walked up and stopped in the doorway. She propped her hands shoulder high on each side of the door and stood looking in, smiling alluringly. She wore heavy makeup and her large bosom rose and fell with each quick breath.

"What y'all talking about?" Her eyes washed over Ashley, burning into his. He looked away. "Hi, baby," she said to Ashley, her voice velvety smooth. "How's my baby?"

"Hey, Bumpsy." Ashley let the front legs of his chair drop to the floor. She walked over and sat in his lap, putting her arms around his neck and hugging and kissing him before he could complete his effort to stand. Having no other place to put his arms but around Bumpsy's waist, Ashley let them hang freely.

Robert, who had stretched his aching joints flat out on the bed just before Bumpsy walked up, said, "Wait a minute. What is this? Should I leave the room or something?"

"This is my man, Robert," Bumpsy said, her eyes in Ashley's.

Robert pretended to get up. "Y'all want to use my bed or something?"

Bumpsy, who was getting nowhere fast with Ashley, stopped her advances, stood up, and bolted over to Robert's bed, lying down beside him. "You love me, don't you, Robert?" she asked wriggling herself up next to him.

"Oooeee!" Robert said. "That's right, baby. Come to daddy and let's get it on."

Still piqued with Ashley, Bumpsy shot to a sitting position beside Robert and rolled her eyes at him. "How you gonna get anything on, all broke up like you is?"

Ashley turned his head and laughed.

"You just put it on me, baby, and see what I can do," Robert said, wriggling his hips as best he could.

Bumpsy glared at Robert disgustedly, scuffled off the crumpled bedspread, and pranced to the door, where she stopped and looked at Ashley long and hard before storming down the hall.

"What in the hell is the matter with you, boy?" Robert said. "She wants you bad."

Ashley looked straight at Robert. "Bumpsy's a married woman."

"What the hell has that got to do with anything?"

"I happen to respect her husband." Ashley rose. "You sure you don't need anything from town?" He looked at his watch. "I'm going to get some books from the school library if old lady Holloway will let me have them. And Harley's got a few books on Negro history I haven't read."

Robert looked at Ashley, his eyes narrowed. "You really mean business about this lawyer stuff, don't you?"

Ashley walked toward the door, stopped, and looked back over his shoulder at Robert. "You just watch me."

"Atta boy," Robert said, slapping his good hand against the bed. I likes to hear you talk like that. Happy birthday, my man!"

A storm was brewing as Ashley gunned the old truck toward home. He glanced up at the thick black clouds sailing along in front of him. He hoped his daddy wouldn't get caught in the storm. He had looked for him in town. But then his daddy might have stopped off and be talking to anybody between home and town, he thought. He hoped those college brochures would soon come. A satisfying feeling enveloped him as he looked at the books on the seat beside him. He glanced up at the sky, thinking of his grandmother, her hopes and dreams for him. College seemed so far away—there were so many obstacles in his path. He looked at the sky. "Let it be soon. Please let it be soon. I've wasted enough time."

The strong wind began to shove the truck from side to side. The storm that was about to happen was like the storm in Ashley's mind that had been brewing since the morning Stoner rushed home from Thomas Rucker's house without the fertilizer.

Breathing heavily, with blood on his hands from having helped the men put Rucker in the car to rush him to the hospital, Stoner had sat down on his front porch step in a daze. Bessie spotted him and came out on the porch. The stunned expression on Stoner's face told Bessie that something was terribly wrong.

"What's the matter, Stoner? What in the world is the matter?" She sat on the step beside him. He stared at the white sandy yard, motionless, his shoulders drooping.

"Lord, Stoner. Tell me what's happened!"

"I've killed him, Bessie. I've killed Mr. Rucker!" He spoke with a voice drained of all its energy. He never took his eyes off the spot he had focused them on in the yard.

Bessie stared wide-eyed at the dry, flaky blood on his hands and began to tremble. "Lord. What in the world happened?"

"He kicked old Sam, Bessie. Kicked him right in the ass with the toe of his shoe and knocked him all the way down the steps—that old man. He fell in a heap at the bottom of the steps. That's all I remember. I couldn't take it. Something exploded in me and

I hit him with every ounce of strength I owned!" He looked around at Bessie. "I'm a man, Bessie. Just because I jumps and says 'yes, suh' and 'no, suh' to him, don't mean I ain't no man—don't mean I can stand by and see my own kind misused." He paused as Bessie put her hand in his and squeezed it. "Ain't no use talking about it no more. I've killed a man, Bessie—a white man."

Bessie rubbed his shoulder, tears welling up in her eyes, and he continued talking. "I could see he was dead when I helped put him in the car; his eyes was closed and he was white as a sheet.... And all that blood!" Stoner paused, took a long breath and, when he exhaled, under the faded-blue denim shirt his muscular shoulders dropped as if it were his last and final breath.

"They kept staring at me, Bessie. All of 'em that had run from the barns and the fields when Miss Rucker started to scream and cry." He looked around at Bessie sitting next to him, clenching her bottom lip. "Do you know what old Ennis said to me, Bessie? While we was waiting for Miss Rucker to come out and throw a blanket over Mr. Rucker on the backseat of the car, he nudged me with his elbow and under his breath said, 'Run, Stoner. Run as fast as you can and as far as you can before the sheriff gets here. Don't never let 'em catch you.'"

Stoner fell silent, looking thoughtfully at the ground, remembering the cruel and degrading manner in which Sheriff Wendy had handled the matter. His gut still wrenched.

Big drops of rain splattered the windshield of the truck as Ashley peered ahead for a glimpse of his father. He spotted a man on a mule and wagon far ahead of him and picked up speed, glad his father was making it in before the storm hit. But when he caught up to the wagon he discovered it was not Stoner but Pappy, an elderly Negro man. Pappy was about to turn off the highway and take the long path up to his house in the field. He heard the truck slowing down behind him and turned. He recognized Ashley and held up two fingers. Ashley stopped completely and let him make his turn, then drove on.

When Ashley drove up in the yard at home the sky was purple. Leaves and twigs swept across the yard, and wind and rain beat him in the face as he ran to the porch.

"Daddy ain't home yet?" he asked Minnie and Eva, who were sitting on the trunk in the front room watching out the window for a glimpse of their father. Minnie looked at Ashley and shook her head *no*, without saying a word.

Ashley went to the kitchen and found Bessie lighting the lamp on the supper table, humming an old hymn.

"I should've got up and carried him to town this morning," he said to Bessie, putting the blame on himself. "He's caught somewhere in this storm. I can crawl faster than that old mule."

Thunder exploded and Bessie winced. "He probably stopped somewhere," she said—for her own benefit as well as Ashley's.

Ashley went back to the front room to watch with

Minnie and Eva. "Here he comes!" he said loudly, and Bessie ran from the kitchen to look.

The wagon was bounding up the path, Stoner standing astride, beating the mule with the lines. As soon as Stoner took care of the mule and wagon, he headed toward the house at a run. Ashley held the door open for him and he ran in, soaking wet, his shirt plastered to his back and rain dripping from the brim of his old felt hat.

"Whew!" Stoner said, as Ashley struggled to close the old weather-beaten door against the strong wind. "I got as far as Snellings's store and thought I'd better stop. After I stayed there awhile it looked like the storm was going around. Then just as soon as I left it got worse."

They all stood looking at him. Bessie handed him a towel and he began drying his face, then dabbing the towel against his wet clothing.

"Go put on some dry clothes," Bessie said to Stoner. "Dinner's ready." She went back to the kitchen to set the table.

Stoner removed a small brown paper sack from the back pocket of his overalls. It contained assorted penny candy. He handed the sack to Minnie. "Y'all divide it up," he said.

He held a package under his arm, wrapped in brown paper and tied with twine thread. Minnie grabbed it from under his arm and ran from the room, Eva following her and giggling. Ashley stood watching but didn't say anything.

By the time they sat down to supper the storm was subsiding. Then when they had finished a special dinner of fried chicken, turnip greens and cornbread, black-eyed peas, and sweet potatoes, Ashley, sitting between Minnie and Eva on the bench at one side of the table, rubbed his hands together vigorously over his supper plate and said, "Now let's get on with the rest of the party. Bring on the cake!"

Minnie glanced at her mother. "What cake? Mama didn't make no cake," she said, looking around at Ashley, a serious look on her face.

"Ah, come on," Ashley said. "I know she made a cake because she was beating on it when I left."

Bessie was smiling as she cleared the supper dishes from the table and set out saucers for everyone. She went to the pie safe and brought back a luscious-looking chocolate cake, placing it in the center of the table. Then she went out on the back porch and dug from under broken pieces of ice a canister of home-made vanilla ice cream.

It had stopped raining and the brilliant red sun lowering itself behind the tall pines was peeping through scattered gray clouds. Bessie had thrown up the kitchen window and cool, damp air, smelling of the cornfield, was circulating through the kitchen, combining with the smell of delicious foods.

Eva looked across the table at Stoner—she had eaten two helpings of cake and ice cream—and said, "Daddy, wasn't that a happy birthday party we gave Ashley?" Then, unable to keep the secret longer, she leaned over and whispered in Ashley's ear, "We got you a birthday present too."

"A present too?" Ashley said in a whisper, looking at Eva, his eyes widened and his mouth open in surprise as he played with her. "Well, let's have it," he said, looking around at Minnie, who was glaring acusingly at Eva for telling.

Minnie got up from the table and walked past Eva, thumping her on the head, on her way to the bedroom. When she came back, she had her hands behind her.

"Close your eyes and put out your hands," she instructed Ashley, while Eva giggled.

Ashley opened his eyes at the touch of the article being placed in his hand. He stared at the red cap.

Stoner watched him staring at it and said, "It was the best one in the store."

Bessie, as well as the others waited for a response. Ashley was thinking, *Did it have to be red? Everybody in the country will know I'm coming.*

"Do you like it, Ashley?" Bessie asked, her elbows propped on the table, her fingers laced under her chin.

All Ashley could think to say was, "This is some hat, man. He took it by the brim and positioned it on his head.

"You been needing a hat out in the field in the hot sun," Bessie said, a pleased look on her face as she rose from the table. Ashley kept taking the hat off and looking at it, thinking, *Why did it have to be red?*

Chapter 7

Mary Jo Rucker slipped on her shortest pink shorts and a strapless little pink thing that barely covered her large bust, which rode high under it. She didn't have to worry about her mother sending her back to her room to change into something decent because Alice had driven into town to get a case of canning jars and she knew it would take the rest of the day for her to drive there and back. But she cringed inside when she thought that her father just might drop by the house before the workday was over and find her down at the barn with Leon. She consoled herself with the thought that he seldom did come back to the house before the workers in the fields had quit and gone home, which was always dusk dark.

She had seen Leon drive by the house on his way down to the barn to work.

She pinned her curly, blonde hair atop her head and looked at herself in the mirror; she assured herself that the style made her look older. Her shapely legs in the full-length mirror looked good, but they were a bit pale; she promised herself that she was going to get a tan. She hunted around on her dresser for the tube of lipstick, blushing pink, that matched what she was wearing. She coated her lips to a hypnotizing pink and then touched just a dab on both cheeks, rubbing it in. She strode into the kitchen and unwrapped the pan of gingerbread left from dinner, cutting a big hunk and wrapping it so she would have an excuse to give Leon for coming down to the barn to see him.

The first time she had mustered the courage to pay Leon a visit down at the barn, she had used the excuse of taking him a tall glass of ice-cold lemonade. Before that, there had been nothing between the two of them except a smile here and there.

Like the day that Leon had knocked on the kitchen door and asked for something to bandage a bleeding finger. She had hurried to the bathroom to get some gauze, bringing along iodine, and had watched him dress his wounded finger out on the back porch. That particular day she had been home alone and welcomed Leon's smiling face and friendly conversation. They had gotten into a conversation about the newborn calves down at the barn. Leon had handed her the iodine and accidentally touched her fingers. It had felt a little awkward but somewhat pleasant—warm—manly....

Then there was the time that Leon had been passing through the yard on his way down to the barn and noticed Mary Jo trying to round up three of her mother's fat brown hens for a big chicken dinner. Leon had stopped his car, slid through the grass, crawled under the house on his knees, got caught under the barbed-wire fence, slipped and slid through the cow pasture, and ended up capturing all three of the hens for Mary Jo. They had laughed together about Leon's determination not to give in to the chickens. Leon had left with a rip in the back of his pants and a skinned elbow.

It had been a few days later that Mary Jo had gone down to the barn with the glass of lemonade.

But the incident that made them turn from being the white girl and the black boy into two warm human beings was the time Mary Jo visited the barn and Leon had his radio plugged in, listening to music while he worked. She had swayed her body to the music while Leon ate the chocolate cake she had taken him. Then a fast song came on and Leon began to show Mary Jo the latest dance he had learned at the Chicken Shack. She giggled while he hurled himself across the floor with a lot of fancy steps, but she was very much impressed with his body movements.

Then a slow piece came on and she admitted that slow dancing was all she had ever done but wasn't very good at that either. That was when Leon volunteered to teach her how to slow-drag. He took her in his strong arms, holding her very gently at first, but his embrace soon tightened. Before long, the two of them were locked into a captivating hold on each other that neither of them cared to break. Then it happened! Leon touched his lips to hers and sent fire burning through every fiber of her being. She tore herself from

Leon's embrace and ran up the path home, afraid that she had stayed at the barn long enough for her mother to be back from her trip to town.

Now she was on her way down to the barn with the piece of gingerbread neatly wrapped and hopefully hidden from view. It was her excuse to go down to see Leon, but she really didn't need an excuse. By now, it was obvious to both of them that they were attracted to each other. However, she was still a white girl and she wanted Leon to understand that she still had some vanity left, thus the gingerbread.

When she first left the house, she hurried along the path, looking straight ahead, reluctant to glance around her for fear of seeing someone spying on her. When she finally got the nerve to search the yard and the surrounding fields with her eyes, she was relieved to see that the way was clear. She would have plenty of time to spend with Leon.

Now as she drew near the barn, she walked swiftly down the path with her bare toes digging into the white sand. She reached up and adjusted her pink halter, which seemed to creep down a little from the weight of her heavy breasts. She could still feel that burning desire she had for Leon when he had touched his lips to hers; now she wanted more.

Mary Jo walked up to the barn door and peered through the screen door at Leon. He was busy whitewashing the walls. His shirt was off and his back was to her. She stood watching him for a few seconds, noticing every muscle in his bare, bronze-colored back each time he swung the brush up and down. She gently opened the screen door and eased inside. Leon heard the sound of the door and turned around. He rushed over to the nail on the wall for his T-shirt. Mary Jo stood smiling at him while he pulled the shirt over his head and smoothed his hand over his disheveled hair.

"You shy devil you," she said to him.

He smiled sheepishly and asked, "What you hiding behind your back?"

"You like gingerbread?"

"Do I? I love it. Can't wait from the time mama makes it until the next time she makes it."

She handed her offering to Leon. "Had lots more than we could eat," she said. Leon's hands were covered with paint, so he ate the gingerbread from the wrapping. Mary Jo stared at his body the whole time.

Leon's heart began to pound a little too fast. *There she was*, he thought, *all his for the taking*. But he couldn't allow himself to look at her; he couldn't permit himself to be tempted. It was much too dangerous. To calm himself, he picked up the brush and began painting again, thinking of what Thomas Rucker would do to him if he caught him making love to his milky-white daughter—him, the black "boy" who worked in his barns. He envisioned blood running all over the place, from Thomas Rucker slashing his body open and leaving him to die a slow death,

Leon continued to brush the whitewash on the wall even when Mary Jo slipped up behind him and her warm fingers began caressing the back of his neck and stroking his hair.

"How did you get all those little waves in your hair?" she asked him, fingering the tiny waves and at the same time easing her body closer to his.

"From brushing," he told her. "My mama told me this morning that I'll go bald before I'm thirty if I keep brushing my hair so much."

As Leon continued painting he could feel Mary Jo's thighs pressing against his buttocks. He could stand it no longer. Suddenly, he wheeled around and grabbed her and kissed her, dropping the paintbrush.

With a moan she collapsed in his arms. Leon eyed the pile of gunnysacks nearby. He ushered her over to them.

They were lying on the sacks making love when they heard a truck come to a screeching halt outside. By the time they heard the door slam they both had jumped up. Leon was certain it was Mary Jo's father coming to kill him. He raced to the window and looked out. To his relief, it was only Stanley, one of the black guys who worked with Leon. He was going toward the barn across from them.

Leon turned back to Mary Jo. When he reached for her she jerked away, saying she had to go and promising to meet him another time. As she hurried up the path toward her house, Leon stood watching her. "That damn Stan," he muttered. "He would have to come at the wrong damn time."

Chapter 8

That Saturday, Slim's Cafe had been pretty quiet all morning but now, in the afternoon, it was beginning to fill with customers, rainy-day customers, since it was a rainy, dreary day. The workers behind the counter knew it was going to be a busy and hectic evening with passersbys stopping in out of the gloomy weather for gossip, music, and some of the best hot dogs, hamburgers, and barbecue sandwiches in town.

A tall pot of homemade chili sat warming on the burner and Clyde Brown was chopping cabbage to fill the big aluminum pan with cole slaw. He would make three or four pans before the day was over.

Daisy Lane had her long black hair neatly tucked behind her head with little pink combs, forcing her bouncing curls to fall straight down the middle of her back. The fresh, starched uniform she wore hugged her shapely body in just the right places to please the male customers who frequented Slim's. She had just run to the powder room and done her makeup again, anticipating the arrival of Ashley Brooks. Each time the door opened her hopes were dashed at the sight of someone else.

The door of the cafe suddenly opened and the place got deathly quiet, leaving only the sound of the music blasting on the jukebox. Heads snapped around and mouths flew open at the sight of the Willis brothers.

Trouble had been brewing between Tank Willis and a guy named Jimmy Foster. It had started the evening before, when Jimmy had been at the Chicken Shack with his girl, Sue. Tank had pulled on Sue one too many times for Jimmy, so he had taken his girl and left to avoid trouble. Then that morning he had run into Tank at the cafe and told him in no uncertain terms to keep his hands off his girl or the next time he wouldn't walk away. An argument ensued and Jimmy ended up giving Tank a bloody nose right there on the spot.

Everyone in the place knew why the Willis brothers had come. The word about Jimmy and Tank's fight had spread pretty fast. Everyone was afraid for Jimmy but still was eager to see what would happen if Jimmy was fool enough to return.

The crowd quickly resumed their chatter and a slow song was playing when Tom Willis chose a stool and ordered a soda, then sat slowly sipping it and letting his eyes burn steadily through Daisy's hips.

Daisy tried to avoid looking in Tom's direction but couldn't help being aware that he was staring at her body. She passed by him with an order of hamburgers when he called to her. "Hey, mama, hows about a little service here?" Daisy tripped over a protruding foot and almost dropped the order she was taking to a booth in the back.

"Just a minute," she said with a trembling voice and pounding heart. All the way back to her customers she was hoping the earth would open up and swallow Tom Willis before she returned. She couldn't bear the thought of being embarrassed before her customers, and she had no doubt that anything the obnoxious Tom said would be offensive or embarrassing. When she got back, she stopped behind the counter, directly across from him. He resumed his hip-staring.

"May I help you?"

"You sure can, pretty thing." His eyes were the eyes of a dissolute person. They told her he would like to do some dirty things to her, but he did not say in words what those things were; all he did was order a hamburger and another soda. It was the fastest order that Daisy had ever made. She hoped he would swallow it whole and get out or die and go to hell, get hit by a truck—anything, as long as he left the cafe.

Clyde had told Daisy all about the trouble brewing between Ashley and the Willis brothers, how Ashley had busted Tank's lip and how the Willis brothers planned to teach the "bully" a lesson. Daisy glanced at Tom Willis eating his hamburger and thought if he laid one finger on her Ashley she would gladly bust a bottle over his ugly head.

Tom Willis had caught Daisy's eyes on him and motioned her to come over to him. She could not be rude to customers, so she responded, walking over to find out what he wanted.

"Yes, may I help you?" she said again. He sat staring at his favorite spot on her body and saying nothing. Daisy was already nervous and she began to tremble a little, anticipating trouble.

"What time do you get off tonight?"

That was not a question Daisy wanted to answer, at least to him. "Me? What time do I get off?" She pointed a trembling finger at her chest, trying to think of an answer that would not offend but not be the truth. He stared at her, as if demanding an answer. "I'm not really sure," she finally answered stiffly. Then she turned and walked away from him.

Lewis Willis walked over from a booth, stopped, and whispered something to Tom. Then Tom got up and the two of them walked toward the door. Tank jumped up and followed them. The three left the cafe. When the door swung shut behind them, Daisy sensed that everyone in the place sighed with relief.

Late that afternoon the drizzling rain stopped and the sun came out. Most of the crowd left the cafe, and Clyde and Daisy were able to take a much-needed break. They were sitting on the customer's side of the counter on stools side by side, Daisy sipping a Pepsi and Clyde eating a barbecue sandwich and drinking a Nehi grape. The door of the cafe suddenly burst open and Clyde's young cousin, Ray, rushed in out of breath, hurried over to Clyde and Daisy, and said, "Did you hear what happened to Jimmy Foster?"

Daisy and Clyde responded simultaneously,

"What?"

"They found Jimmy lying over in the alley by the pool hall, unconscious and all bloody and everything!"

Clyde and Daisy looked at each other and Daisy's eyes teared up. She felt sorry for Jimmy, but she was also deathly afraid of what Tom Willis might do to Ashley.

Ray continued: "Jimmy said later that he didn't know who attacked him because he was jumped from behind."

Again Daisy and Clyde looked at each other.

Rosa Eatman stood in the dirt road that led up to Bessie's house looking at her bloody knee and wondering what to do about Leonard. It was late Saturday afternoon and she was hot from the sun and the exertion of running. She was also in pain. Hurrying to get away from Leonard, she had stumbled over a rock jutting from the path and scraped her knee.

She looked back and didn't see Leonard coming after her, so she gathered her skirt in her hands and, holding it away from her knee, she hobbled on up toward Bessie's house.

Leonard had come in from work that day and found his supper still cooking on the stove instead of being on the table, and this had set him into a tailspin. Lately he had been getting much worse; the least little thing seemed to cause him to lose complete control of his temper. Not only would he argue with Rosa, but he would often explode and end up slamming his fist against her jaw. Afterwards he would become as meek as a lamb, but he never apologized. It had gotten so bad that Rosa was now actually afraid of him. Sometimes during his rages she wished he was dead, but after it was all over and he was sitting quietly at the table eating after a hard day in the field, she felt guilty and even sorry for wishing such a thing.

Rosa had begun to sense when Leonard was about to become violent, and she would stop whatever she was doing and get away from him until he had calmed down. A few minutes ago after he had grabbed her arm and had drawn back his fist preparing to strike her, she had pulled away from him and run away.

Now, walking on up the road, she hated to face Bessie's children, with their somber, sympathetic stares. And Ashley—she didn't know how much more he would take of seeing her abused. She prayed that Leonard wouldn't follow her to try to take her back home.

Rosa knocked loudly on Bessie's door, then went inside calling out to Bessie.

Ashley was getting ready to drive to town when he heard Rosa run in calling Bessie. He met her and looked down at her bleeding knee, then at the tears running down her face. He knew what was happening. He didn't say a word but just walked on past her to the door and stood looking down the path.

Bessie took Rosa in hand and tended to her knee. "It's just scraped," Rosa said, then broke down again. "Bessie, something's happening to Leonard. I don't know what to do!"

Ashley left the door to examine Rosa's injured knee and to look at her face for bruises. While he did so, Minnie and Eva stood watch with rapidly pounding hearts. "Here he comes!" Minnie said, and Eva began to cry, afraid for her aunt.

Ashley started back to the door, then turned to Rosa. "Don't worry, Aunt Rosa," he said, "Uncle Leonard's hit you for the last time. I'll take care of him."

Bessie stared at Ashley as if wanting to protest, and Minnie and Eva tugged at his pants, trying to get him away from the door, but Ashley wouldn't budge.

Leonard hit the door with his fist. "Open this motherfucking door," he yelled. Ashley swung the door open and Leonard started to storm in but found Ashley blocking his path.

"Where is she?" Leonard asked, a wild-looking expression on his face; Ashley had never seen him in such a frantic state.

"What's wrong with you, Uncle Leonard?" Ashley asked, continuing to block his way each time he tried to pass him. "This don't make no kind of sense. You know Aunt Rosa don't deserve this kind of treatment."

Leonard ignored him and tried to get past again, but Ashley shoved him back by his shoulders.

"Get your motherfucking hands off me!" Leonard said. "And git out of my goddamned way." He lunged forward, and Ashley grabbed him and pinned him against the wall. Leonard didn't try to fight Ashley, and Ashley continued to try to reason with him.

"Uncle Leonard, have you lost your mind? You're acting like you've got no sense at all. You've got no reason to keep beating on Aunt Rosa. It ain't right, and you know it."

Leonard only stared at Ashley, as if shocked by the fact that he was talking to him so calmly. But the words of reason seemed to reach him eventually. After a few minutes Leonard broke down and began to cry. Then, through his tears and sobs, he said, "I don't mean to hurt nobody, Ashley. Specially not Rosa; I love Rosa, but I'm in terrible pain, and I'm scared."

"What is it, Uncle Leonard? Where does it hurt?"

"My head, but it's not just a headache. It's something…, I don't know, Ashley. Help me, boy. You've got to help me to get to a doctor. I can't stand this pain much longer!"

Ashley and Rosa sat in the waiting room at Dr. Evans's office while the doctor examined Leonard. All the way to town Leonard had moaned from the excruciating pain in his head. When Dr. Evans came to the door, Rosa looked up at him anxiously. He motioned for her to come into his office. Once Rosa was seated in front of Dr. Evans's desk, he informed her that he wanted Leonard admitted to the hospital immediately. He had suffered a severe stroke by the time the doctor got him on the examining table and he was now unconscious.

Rosa looked back toward the hospital and began crying again as Ashley drove away. Leonard was dead from a cerebral hemorrhage.

Now she was heading home without Leonard. *What am I going to do?* she wondered, crying softly while Ashley tried to console her. She hadn't been away from him one single night during the twenty years they had been married. She thought of all the busted lips and swollen eyes he had giver her, and she thought of the loneliness waiting for her in that little secluded house far back up in the field. She wondered—truly wondered—if she hadn't rather have Leonard back, temper and beatings and all.

Ashley offered to take Rosa by Slim's Cafe for something to eat, but the thought of food made her stomach turn. She remained outside in the truck while Ashley went in to get something for himself, telling her that he intended to bring her something anyway; she could eat it later at home.

For the third time that day Daisy had gone back to the little powder room in back of the cafe and stood before the dull mirror to freshen her makeup, hoping Ashley would come by as he did almost every Saturday.

When Ashley pushed open the cafe door and walked in, Daisy's heart leaped into her throat. She wanted to shout, *Where have you been all day*? Ashley smiled and said hello and immediately ordered two hamburgers and a grape drink.

Out of the corner of her eye, she watched him eat. That strong chin line, she thought, those broad shoulders. She must have wiped the counter a hundred times as an excuse to look over at him, sitting there eating, his bronze face solemn, his curly hair parted and neatly combed back. She even delighted in seeing his adam's apple jiggle as he turned the bottled drink up to his mouth and drank thirstily.

After Ashley finished eating, he ordered a barbecue sandwich and hot black coffee to go. Daisy waited as he rose from the stool to take out his wallet. She smelled the faint odor of after-shave and leather. His smell. It sent chills up her spine. She watched him walk out, his usual slow-but-steady gait, like a man who knew where he was going and why. The rest of Daisy's evening collapsed at her feet.

Rosa accepted the coffee but told Ashley to give the sandwich to Eva. Night settled in all around them as they left the town square and took the open highway, headed toward home.

After they had driven for a bit, Rosa looked over at Ashley and asked curiously, "Don't Jim Lane's daughter work in Slim's Cafe?"

"You mean Daisy?" Ashley asked.

"Yes," Rosa said. "Jim Lane is Leonard's cousin. I was surprised to hear that she was working in a place like that, being a nice, quiet girl like she is, and how her mama and daddy keep such close watch over her. Jim hardly ever lets her out of his sight, least he didn't used to."

"She's a nice girl," Ashley said, looking thoughtfully at the headlights shining on the road. "And a pretty one too."

Chapter 9

"I'll meet you Saturday night," Mary Jo told Leon. She had sneaked down to the barn late that Friday evening before Leon got off work for the weekend.

Mary Jo's mother often let her spend Saturday night with her friend Sue Ellen. Leon knew where it was. They made plans to meet down the dark lonely road from Sue Ellen's house.

That Saturday night when Leon parked and sat looking up through the field for Mary Jo to come running down the long path, he feared for his life. He could be lynched.

Leon saw someone coming and held his breath until he recognized Mary Jo.

"Thought you'd changed your mind," Leon said. "Thought you'd chickened out."

"I had to wait until Sue Ellen's mother and father left. They went to a sitting-up. They won't be back 'til way late." She breathed a sigh of relief. "I thought they'd never leave!" Then, as Leon eased the car on down the road, he relaxed beside her.

They went for a long drive, Leon steering clear of any public place where there were people. Even the blacks would object to Leon's associating with a white girl, because when whites got in a lynching mood these days, they would pick on any black person around. Leon and Mary Jo both knew what they were up against. But they liked each other, were physically attracted to each other, and the threat of it all made it more exciting to be together.

Ashley's friends could now recognize him from a distance, by his red cap. "Man, you can see that cap a mile away," they would laugh and say.

Ashley would smile; he wore it only to please his mother. One morning he had stopped by Snellings's store and set his cap on the counter while he drank a soda and talked to Mr. Snellings. When he walked out, he forgot and left the cap on the counter. The cap was so recognizable that Mr. Snellings knew who it belonged to, and he kept it for Ashley until the next time he came in.

Stoner's trial was to begin tomorrow. Before supper Ashley tried once again to get Stoner to talk about what the outcome of the trial might be, as well as the family's prospects for the future. He and Ashley were sitting on the front porch waiting for Bessie to call them to supper, although neither of them had much of an appetite.

"There's nothing to talk about, Ashley," Stoner said. "I split open a white man's skull and it took eighteen stitches to close it back up. Ain't too much hope for a black man that's got this kind of trouble facing him."

"But Mr. Rucker provoked you, Daddy," Ashley said sharply. "You went out of your mind for a minute."

"You think an all-white jury's gonna understand how I felt when I saw that helpless old man fall in a heap at the bottom of the steps?" Stoner said. "No!"

That evening at the supper table Ashley watched Stoner pushing his biscuit through the molasses on his plate, a faraway look in his eyes. And Bessie kept excusing herself from the table to go mop away the tears that were welling up in her eyes.

Minnie anxiously tried to keep a pleasant conversation going despite the black cloud that hung over the table, saying things like: "Daddy, I fed the hogs already. You won't have to do that. Do you know that old sow with the ring in her nose? Well, she's the meanest thing you ever saw. Thinks every ear of corn you chunk over in the pen belongs to her."

With no one paying attention to her, Eva sank half a biscuit in her glass of water, watching it swell double, and was about to attack the whole mess with a spoon until Minnie noticed and snatched the spoon from her hand.

After the rest of the family had gone to bed Ashley, unable to sleep, eased out on the front porch and sat on the top step in his underwear.

The sky was storm-threatening gray and a cool

breeze was stirring. He sat with his head back letting the breeze bathe his apprehensive body. The frogs and crickets were silent and the only sound was the rumble of thunder. He felt totally helpless in this situation. He wanted desperately to believe that Mr. Taylor would see that Stoner would get a fair trial, but Mr. Taylor was a white man. Ashley believed his father would stand a better chance if he had his own kind defending him.

Even though there were no Negro lawyers in their area, Ashley was aware that some existed. He had read as much information on them as he could get his hands on.

The first of his race to be formally admitted to the bar in the United States was Marcus B. Allen, who had passed his legal examination in Worcester, Massachusetts, and had been admitted in 1845.

"We need our own kind representing us," Ashley muttered. He sighed, looking out toward the cornfield into the darkness. "If only I could...."

Ashley realized getting a law degree under any circumstances took time; in his case, he knew it was going to be an uphill battle all the way. It would soon be the beginning of September. He should already have made his application and known whether or not he had been accepted. Ashley knew, because of the trouble his father was in, that he was going to set aside his dreams temporarily. But the sense of helplessness he felt did not discourage him; it merely reinforced his determination to succeed, so that his people would have him to represent them in the law courts one day. *I'm going to be the best damn lawyer that ever set foot in a courtroom*, he swore silently to himself.

Sitting there in the quiet he thought of his grandmother, could see her face, could almost see the movement of her lips, speaking to him, encouraging him.

Ashley glanced at the sky, "Well, tomorrow's the day," he muttered. "I'm leaving it all in your hands." He got up and went to bed.

The day of Stoner's trial was the first day of September, the day they all wished would never come, and at the same time wanted it to hurry and be over with.

Ashley awakened to the drone of rain hitting the roof and the sides of the house, making a sad day even sadder. He lay motionless for a few minutes, watching the drops trickle down the windowpane. It wouldn't be long before Mr. Peterson would come to pick them up and take them to the courthouse.

When Stoner was dressed and ready, he went to stand on the front porch to wait for the others. Stoner wore a brand-new white shirt and the blue tie that Ashley had given him for Christmas. He wore the dark blue dress pants Mr. Peterson had given him that had belonged to Peterson's brother, and he wore his Sunday brown shoes. His hair was parted and neatly combed back. He stood frowning; the small scar on his forehead narrowed, as he looked thoughtfully through the rain.

Bessie dressed Eva and sent her out on the porch to wait with Stoner. Eva walked up to her father and took his callused hand in hers and began to swing it back and forth. "You like my new dress, Daddy?" she asked, looking up at Stoner, a glint of pride in her young, innocent eyes.

Stoner looked down at his youngest child and, moving back some to get a better look, said, "That's real pretty." He reached over and caressed her head.

"I know it is," Eva said and ran from underneath Stoner's large hand to the end of the porch, where she began to catch rain in her palm.

Stoner stared out at the field of tall ripe corn across from the house and wondered if he would be there to help Ashley harvest it. At this season all of the farmers and their families were extremely busy grading and tying tobacco for the market. Tobacco-selling time had to be the highlight of the year for the farmers. Each time they sold a load of tobacco they got a few dollars in their pockets. They had already dug sweet potatoes, and hog-killing time was coming up; in his thoughts, Stoner could almost smell the chitterlings cooking on the stove then. At Christmastime there would be plenty of fresh meat and plenty of sweet potatoes for candied yams and pies. Thanksgiving and Christmas were times they looked forward to, the pie safe stacked with pies and cakes, friends and relatives congregating and having fun.

Stoner looked down at the porch and rubbed the back of his neck. "Lord, we do have our hard times," he muttered, "but there's some good times too. A man never fully appreciates what he's got till it's taken away from him." He walked over and sat on a twine-bottom chair, and immediately Eva ran up and sat on his knee.

"Daddy, the wheel came off my wagon yesterday. Will you fix it when we come back from town?" She was looking up into his face and at the same time plaiting his fingers.

"Yes, honey. Daddy'll fix your wagon when we get back," Stoner said, turning his head so Eva couldn't see the tears in his eyes.

Ashley, wearing a white shirt and tie and dress pants, walked to the front door and stood looking at Eva on Stoner's lap. Sensitive to his serious stare, Eva got up and went into the house.

Ashley walked over to the edge of the porch and stood looking out at the rain. A few minutes of ringing silence dragged by before he spoke.

"Soon be time for us to cut that corn," Ashley said pensively. "I'll be glad, so we can see down to the road again."

Without looking around, Stoner said, "You've got to face it, Ashley. I might not be here to help you get that corn in..., or do nothing else, for that matter." His voice cracked with emotion.

Ashley turned to face him, frowning. "Now, what kind of talk is that?" He went over and gave Stoner a consoling slap on the shoulder. "You gonna be right back here with us this evening eating some of the blackberry pie Ma cooked up for our dinner."

Stoner didn't respond, only kept his eyes focused on the rain beating down on the yard.

Chapter 10

Moses Fitzgerald Taylor, attorney-at-law, was a graduate of Harvard law school. He was a tall, heavy-set man, fifty-six-years-old. His deep green eyes conveyed a burning inner drive, which few people understood. He was known for his skillful questioning and for holding his juries spellbound with his eloquent summations.

He was the son of a North Carolina cotton planter. As a young man, during breaks from law school, he would visit back home and walk down to the edge of the cotton field—standing dressed in a fine suit and tie, cupping a hand over his eyes to shield them from the blinding sun—to watch the black backs bent to the broiling sun, dragging their cotton sacks behind them, fervently plucking the precious commodity from the bolls. Taylor acquired an unusual appreciation for black labor, fully realizing it was directly responsible for the financing of his education. Having witnessed how hard they worked and realizing how limited their opportunities were, he harbored a heartfelt sympathy for blacks, which was why he was a great supporter of the National Association for the Advancement of Colored People.

Taylor himself owned a big tobacco farm in Mason County and kept a small law office in the town, taking cases there that specially interested him, though most of his law practice was in the city.

In this particular criminal case, Taylor was defending a black charged with assault to commit murder.

Most bosses were not villains out of an old-fashioned melodrama but simply men of their times, struggling to get along while treating their black workers as well as could be expected. But there existed still some men like Thomas Rucker who were mean and insensitive, even cruel in their treatment of blacks.

Inside the courtroom, Judge Malcolm Skipwith took the bench. He was a tall, stocky man, with black eyebrows that resembled woolly caterpillars. The United States flag stood behind his right shoulder, and the witness stand and the jury box were to his left.

The seating for the spectators was similar to that of a small church, but of course the spectators were segregated. The whites sat in shiny brown pews in the center section, facing the judge, and there was a separate section set off to the side at a right angle for the blacks. They faced the whites on their left and the judge on their right. A hip-high banister separated the black spectators from the whites.

In front of the judge's bench, there were two separate tables for the prosecution and defense. Moses Taylor and his client, the defendant Stoner Brooks, were positioned to the left of Judge Skipwith, and Mifford Rockingham, the district attorney, and Thomas Rucker at a table to the right of him.

Rockingham was a tall, lean man with a beak nose and a facial twitch that made his left eye wink uncontrollably. Being district attorney for a wide area of the state and living outside the county, he was not as well known to the townspeople as Moses Taylor was, since he was seen there only when district court convened in Mason.

This did not matter to Thomas Rucker and the majority of the whites, for they believed the outcome of this trial was a foregone conclusion, that Stoner Brooks was headed straight for jail.

Taylor tried to keep the obvious racists off the jury by using his ten peremptory challenges, though he knew that it would be impossible to get a truly impartial jury. The twelve men seated in the jury box would all be white, and it was an inescapable fact that they would be grounded in the tradition of the black codes of the South. One of the rules of the black codes, which had been set in southern culture in the years after the Civil War, was that blacks were not allowed to strike whites even in self-defense. It was even a crime to use insulting language toward a white man.

Taylor had prepared Stoner's defense fully realizing that he could not rely entirely on strict interpretation of the law and demand that the jury recognize Stoner's civil rights. He had to plead directly to the hearts and consciences of the individual men on the jury for Stoner's freedom.

Mifford Rockingham rose to his feet to begin the opening statement for the prosecution. He wore a tan suit with the sleeves too short, and a white shirt and a pea-green tie. "First of all I would like to thank you men for being here," Rockingham said to the jury. "I know how busy you are this time of year, trying to get your tobacco ready for market and all. But this won't take long. I promise you, this is a cut-and-dried case."

His eyes shot to Stoner Brooks and the eyes of the jurors automatically followed him.

"The defendant over there is Stoner Brooks. He is accused of assaulting his white boss with his fist, splitting open his scalp, which took eighteen stitches to close. Mr. Thomas Rucker almost bled to death before they could get him to the hospital."

Rockingham's left eye winked rapidly as he expounded on Stoner Brooks's vicious attack on his white boss. "We all know, gentlemen, that we cannot allow this kind of barbarism from our colored workers." He paced up and down before the jury, stabbing the air with his finger and warning them that if they let Stoner Brooks get away with this, they might as well kiss white supremacy good-bye.

Bessie and Ashley sat side by side in the colored section of the courtroom. Bessie was wearing her blue and white dress and blue straw hat that had faded purple. Her hair was straightened and curled. She listened to the low murmur of the white spectators whispering to each other, commenting approvingly on what

Rockingham was saying, and she could feel the hostility rising. She took a deep breath and her eyes fell upon the long window behind the jury box. Outside it was still raining and the green foliage on the trees gently swayed under the force of the downpour. Bessie felt as helpless as those drenched leaves; she sat tightly coiling her handkerchief around her forefinger, her heart going out to Stoner.

Ashley sat erect, his eyes studying the stern faces of the jurors, trying to analyze their reactions. *Christ Jesus*! he thought. *Will Mr. Taylor be able to make these men understand*? He looked at his father sitting motionless beside Moses Taylor, his face calm, with only a trace of the fear and turmoil he was feeling visible in his eyes.

Rockingham had the jury; Ashley just knew it. They were nodding their heads and agreeing with everything he was saying.

In finishing his opening remarks Rockingham said, "Gentlemen, we southerners desperately need to maintain respect and obedience of our colored help. You must set an example with this case, send a message to any Negro who might be tempted to raise his hand against his employer that we will not tolerate this kind of behavior. If you do not nip this kind of savagery in the bud, you might as well shut down your farms and move to the North." He thanked them and took his seat.

Moses Taylor rose to address the jury. He wore a beige suit, a crisp white shirt, a dark-brown tie, and expensive shoes. His thick auburn hair, parted and wavy, was white at the temples.

"If Your Honor please," he said, then turned to the jurors. "Gentlemen, gone are the days when profit-sharing overseers, interested only in getting as many hours of work and as large a crop out of the Negro workers as possible, can nail a black man to the side of the barn by his ear, or string him up by his wrist and flog him...." He looked straight at Thomas Rucker. "...or kick him down a flight of steps, and not expect retaliation." With each word he spoke, his voice rose slightly, growing gradually louder and sharper, prompting the jurors and the spectators to listen in expectation.

The courtroom was now deathly quiet, with all eyes glaring at the defense attorney.

Moses Taylor turned and looked at Stoner Brooks. "This man, gentlemen, is a good husband and father, who has never been in trouble with the law a day in his life until now. He is charged here with assault to commit murder on his white boss, Mr. Thomas Rucker. But I tell you, gentlemen, Thomas Rucker caused this assault upon himself as surely as if he had reached out and grabbed Stoner Brooks's fist and slammed it against his own head. Yes, Stoner Brooks did strike Thomas Rucker. And it was not in self-defense; it was out of self-respect. And I tell you now that any black man, under identical circumstances, would have done the same thing."

Moses Taylor rubbed his chin while he stared thoughtfully down at the floor. "I ask you to remember one thing: under the law of this state, the prosecution must prove beyond any reasonable doubt that the act of assault and battery was not provoked. And before the trial is over we will present solid evidence to show you that Stoner Brooks's assault upon Thomas Rucker was absolutely, without a doubt, unavoidable. Thank you."

The witnesses for the prosecution began with Thomas Rucker taking the stand to tell the court his side of the story. He wore a pair of khaki pants, a white shirt and navy tie, and a brand-new pair of brogans. His eyes were sharp daggers slicing Stoner Brooks up and down as he spoke. "We white men have got to maintain control and discipline over our workers, black and white." Then he turned to direct his words to the white spectators. "And nigra men have got to learn that they just don't get up in a white man's face."

"Objection, Your Honor," Taylor said. "The witness is expressing his opinions, not stating facts. Would you please direct the witness to stick to telling what happened on his back porch that morning?"

Judge Skipwith looked down at Thomas Rucker. "The witness will tell what happened on his back porch that morning."

Thomas Rucker, his thin blond hair slicked back and the pink of his scalp showing through, directed his steel-blue eyes at the floor and hoisted himself further back in the witness chair.

"Sam Jones, the old nigra man that works around my house doing odd jobs said I promised him a ham for painting my kitchen. I didn't remember promising him no ham. I told him after he finished, to take the piece of side meat and go on home, but he kept insisting on me giving him a ham. I don't know what got into Sam. He'd never acted like that before. Finally I got tired arguing with him and told him to get on off the porch and go on home. That's when he waved his finger in my face. Well that made me pretty goddamn mad and I knocked his hand out of my face." Thomas Rucker paused briefly and then said, "He must have lost his balance or something. The next thing I knowed he was laying at the bottom of the steps, and here comes Stoner Brooks sailing up on my porch and slamming his fist against my head. He didn't have a goddamned thing to do with it!" Thomas Rucker looked over at Stoner and his eyeballs quivered with hatred.

The next witness was Sheriff Wendy, who had been called to the Rucker home after the incident. He said that there was so much blood on the porch that he was certain Thomas Rucker was already dead.

Then Dr. Witherspoon, who had tended Thomas Rucker at the hospital, testified, followed by two other white men who worked for Rucker.

Each time Rockingham finished with a witness, he turned to Moses Taylor and said, "Your witness."

In cross-examining one of Thomas Rucker's white workers, an elderly man who had a face like a weasel, Moses Taylor asked, "Mr. Aikens, is it true that Thomas Rucker flung a hammer at the head of one of his white workers in a fit of anger, missing him by only a few inches? And that man had him prosecuted in this very courtroom?"

The man answered yes, but when Taylor was finished cross-examining Aikens, Rockingham directed further questions to the witness, and by the time he was finished, he had made it seem as though, without that one little incident, Thomas Rucker was one of God's Apostles.

When Rockingham rested his case, Moses Taylor called four prominent white landowners to the stand to testify to Stoner Brooks's character. All four of them said Stoner was one of the finest men they had ever known and that they would be proud to have him as a tenant on their farm. Then Stoner Brooks took the witness stand.

"I went up to Mr. Rucker's that morning to get a bag of fertilizer and tied the mule to the tree and walked toward the back porch. Mr. Rucker and Mr. Sam was standing on the porch arguing about something. I stopped and started to turn around and go back, but I needed the fertilizer that morning. It wasn't none of my business. I hated I had come up on them like that. But, like I said, I wanted to ask Mr. Rucker for a bag of fertilizer. I stopped there and waited. Everything else happened like Mr. Rucker said it did, 'cept Mr. Sam didn't lose his balance and fall down the steps. He'd already give up on getting the ham and was starting down the steps, when Mr. Rucker got real mad, like he sometimes does, and hauled off and kicked Mr. Sam in the rear end with all his might, like he was a dog or something. And Mr. Sam went tumbling down the steps and fell on the ground in a heap."

Stoner swallowed hard, and for the first time locked eyes with Thomas Rucker. "When I saw that old man laying down there in the dirt trying to get to his feet, something just went off in my head and before I knowed what happened I'd hit Mr. Rucker. Right behind him there on the porch was an old iron stove that he hauled out of his kitchen when he got the new one, and he fell backwards and hit his head on the corner of it."

"Your witness," Taylor said to Rockingham.

"No cross-examination," Rockingham said.

"I would like to call John Peterson to the stand," Taylor announced.

John Peterson rose and moved toward the witness box, his old brown felt hat in his hand. He took the oath and sat down.

Rockingham wondered what Moses Taylor hoped to accomplish by having another white man repeat the same thing about Stoner Brooks. He knew he had won the case—knew he had won it even before anybody set foot in the courthouse that morning.

"Mr. Peterson, would you tell the court what you know about Stoner Brooks?"

"I been knowing Stoner and his family for almost twenty years now," Peterson said, pinching the fold of his hat together. "Like these other gentlemen said, Stoner Brooks is a good man. They don't come no better."

"Do you happen to know Stoner Brooks's son, Mr. Peterson?"

"Yeah, I know Ashley. He's worked for me on the side since he was eleven years old. He's one of the finest young men I've ever come in contact with."

"Would you say that Ashley and his father are similar in character?"

"I believe that when it comes to love of your fellow man Ashley and Stoner Brooks are as much alike as any two human beings can be."

"Mr. Peterson, in order to give the court some idea of the kind of humanitarianism we're talking about here, would you tell the court what happened one morning this past August?"

Peterson drew a long breath and forced it out, permitting himself to concentrate on what happened that morning. "Me and Ashley had to go down to the river to cut some logs that morning."

"Speak louder, Mr. Peterson, so the court can hear you," Judge Skipwith said.

Peterson had tried to push this incident to the back of his mind, but it still came back to haunt him from time to time. It was painful talking about it.

"Me and Ashley had to go down to the river to cut a load of logs that morning," Peterson said loudly and clearly. "My son, John, who is twelve, begged me to let him go with us. I didn't want him to go nowhere near that river. John's such a busybody. He's a good boy, but he's always getting into things, kind of adventuresome, I guess you could say. He kept begging to go and I finally gave in.

"At lunchtime we all sat down on some sacks there by a tree to eat. John finished eating first and got up and started wandering around picking up rocks. Me and Ashley took our time finishing eating, resting, and talking.

"I'd warned John time after time how dangerous that river was, so I didn't worry too much when I noticed he was out of sight. I figured he was right there nearby. But after a few minutes when he hadn't come back, I was just about to call him when I heard these screams coming from the woods toward the river. I froze in my tracks, my legs so weak I could hardly move.

"Me and Ashley struck out through the woods, Ashley in front of me. We didn't have time to find the path leading to the river so we plowed through the thicket, briars grabbing our skin and limbs poking us in the face, till we got to John.

"A big black snake had come up behind John and scared him. He had fallen down the side of the riverbank and was clutching a little bush, screaming every breath, his eyes peeled wide with fear.

"I looked at that big black river getting ready to swallow up my boy and cried, 'God, have mercy! I can't swim!' Just then the bush uprooted and John disappeared under that black water!

"I ran as far down the bank as I could go without falling in, crying, 'God, have mercy! God have mercy.' Just then I heard something dash past me like lightning and I saw Ashley plunge headfirst into the river."

Peterson slipped his handkerchief from his pocket and dabbed at the tears in his eyes, despite his efforts to fight them back. He continued: "Ashley stayed under that water for what seemed like a lifetime. Then I saw him pop us, struggling for breath, but no John. I knew I'd never see my son alive again. Then Ashley went back and this time stayed down even longer. But when he popped back up this time he had John under his arm. Ashley hoisted John up on the side of the bank and commenced to give him artificial respiration. John was in bad shape, but Ashley got him to breathing all right."

Peterson looked over and his eyes met Ashley's. He pointed a finger at Ashley for all the spectators to see. "I'll be in debt to that young man till the day I die."

Moses Taylor, standing with his forefinger pressed against his lips, looking down at the floor, a sad expression on his face, turned to Rockingham. "Your witness."

Rockingham listened to the hush that had fallen over the courtroom. He challenged Peterson's testimony, objected strongly to its admissibility. "It has nothing to do with the man's guilt or innocence."

"Indeed it only points indirectly to Stoner's good character, through a statement that the son is like the father," Taylor replied.

Taylor then explained that he intended to show how Ashley's rescue of John Peterson was simply following his father's example. He told of an incident when Stoner was a young boy, around Ashley's age, and had saved a white friend from a burning house. Stoner still had a small scar on his forehead from this incident.

The jury stayed out for two hours. Bessie and Ashley remained glued to their seats. Bessie sat on the edge of the seat, her legs crossed at the ankles. There was a weary expression on her face as she clutched her pocketbook on her knees.

"Lord, have mercy," she said to Ashley. "It's taking them so long. I don't know how much more I can take. Lord, what in the world are they going to do? Things just don't change overnight."

Ashley uncrossed his legs, shifted from the left hip

to the right, and crossed his legs again. "Change got to come sometimes. This might be the time."

They looked and saw the jury filing back into the room, the same bitter and vengeful expressions on their faces as they had worn during the trial.

Judge Skipwith cleared his throat. "Has the jury reached a verdict?"

"It has, Your Honor."

The judge nodded and his clerk walked over to the foreman of the jury, took a slip of paper from him, and handed it to the judge.

Judge Skipwith studied the slip of paper in his hand; then his eyes slowly moved around the courtroom, stopping briefly on Rockingham, moving on to Moses Taylor, and then finally settling on Stoner Brooks.

"The defendant will please rise."

Stoner took a deep breath, hesitated, and then got to his feet slowly, as though he had been drained of all his energy. His eyes fell to the floor and remained there, like those of a condemned man.

Judge Skipwith read from the slip of paper, "This jury finds the defendant, Stoner Brooks, innocent of assault to murder but guilty of simple assault. The court fines him twenty dollars."

When Bessie got to Stoner her hat had shifted to the side of her head like a drunken woman. She grabbed Stoner and stood hugging him and softly crying. Ashley walked up to his father and hugged him tightly, and then kept slapping him on the back like someone trying to help a child who was choking on a piece of food.

Chapter 11

The melodious voices of young children playing tag, hide-and-seek, and red-light rang out across the open grounds like an inharmonious choir. Women with starched white aprons over their Sunday dresses unloaded baskets of home-cooked food from trucks and cars and wagons. In the cool, refreshing shade of spreading oaks, men hurried to finish making the long table from planks and sawhorses that would be draped with white sheets for tablecloths.

It was the Saturday afternoon of the church picnic, which was being held in the clearing by the pond. It was a heaven-sent affair for the Brooks family, giving them the opportunity to sweep behind them the unpleasantness that had haunted them for weeks.

When the table was all finished and draped in white and loaded with food, it stood in mouth-watering splendor, stretched across the green grass like a giant white snake, its tablecloth flapping in the breeze.

The different varieties of foods—dish against dish from one end of the long table to the other—were all ready for the taking—that is, after the Reverend James Edwards said grace. While Reverend Edwards tried to quiet the big crowd so he could say grace, the salivary glands of the grownups were working double-time, and the excited youngsters were having to be restrained with firm hands.

At both ends of the table sat tubs of home-cooked pork barbecue. The barbecuing had been done over at Brother Lucas's home the night before. Stoner and four other deacons of the church had nurtured the roasting pigs until the early hours of the morning, occasionally turning the two carcasses lying on wire screens stretched over pits of red-hot coals, and constantly swabbing on the homemade barbecue sauce. Then the finished product, tender and juicy, with just the right spicy flavor, had been finely chopped. Over in Brother Lucas's backyard at that very moment the coals still smoldered in the pits.

The first category of food on the table, starting at the left end, where the line of people began, was the salads, bowls and bowls of white and yellow potato salad, garnished with sliced boiled eggs and pickles and tomatoes, as well as practically any other kind of salad anyone could want. Then came the pans of crisp, golden fried chicken, and country hams, boiled and baked and garnished with red cherries and pineapple slices, the ham sliced an inch thick, so tender it melted in the mouth. Then came the cornbread, fried patties, golden muffins, and crispy pones. Homemade buttermilk biscuits and yeast rolls came next, and then the greens, turnip greens, butterbeans, collard greens, cabbages, field peas, and blackeyed peas, all cooked country style, with little purple chunks of seasoning meat gracing the tops of the bowls.

The most exciting section of food on the table was the dessert. Each church member had baked her specialty; it gave the women a chance each year to show off their baking hands. Of all the cakes, chocolate, coconut, pineapple, orange, and caramel, the chocolate seemed to "take the cake."

But pie lovers had no trouble finding their favorites among the coconut cream, chocolate, pecan, lemon meringue, and the all-time favorite sweet potato.

To wash down the delicious foods, there was a big barrel of ice-cold lemonade, dipped up by a smiling brother of the church.

The over-stuffed stomachs were crying for mercy even before dessert.

After everyone finished eating, the crowd scattered to different activities, and the ladies began to tackle the difficult task of cleaning up the leftovers.

"Here, Miss Nellie," Bessie Brooks said. "Since you like these pickles so much, why don't you take this jar on home with you. And if you don't mind, I sure would like that leftover jar of pickled peaches. You do make the best I've ever put my mouth on."

The evening sunlight sparkled on the shimmering pond as eager fishermen stood motionless, waiting patiently for a nibble. The sound of horseshoes being tossed against spikes rang out across the clearing like the constant tolling of a high-pitched bell, while bombastic players with deft fingers strove for absolute contact between the two pieces of metal.

Out on the baseball diamond, exultant shouts rose high and then slowly faded in the breeze when a man slid to home base, head first, leaving a big cloud of yellow dust hanging in the air.

Ashley sat on the back of the pickup, dangling his feet and munching on a slice of sweet potato pie. His shirt was open to his navel and sweat poured down his temples. His pant legs were rolled up, and the dust covering his shoes was as thick as that on his eyebrows. He had just beaten Bucky at a game of horseshoes.

Ashley looked and saw his younger sister, Eva, darting in and out of a group of children as some boy chased her. Ashley smiled at her having fun, after what the family had endured. He looked around for Minnie but didn't see her. He became uneasy. Minnie was a beautiful girl. Right away he began to think anxious thoughts. Had some older boy lured her somewhere?

Then he saw her down by the pond with a group of teenagers. She was standing talking to Buddyboy Hall. He watched her for a few minutes, no longer wearing the braid down her back, her hair swept atop her head. He realized for the first time that his precious little sister was growing up. Their mother had done her job well raising them. Minnie could take care of herself without him looking over her shoulder.

Ashley was thankful to see a look of happiness return to Stoner's eyes, and he was himself again, laughing and joking at the picnic. Ashley had played a game of horseshoes with him and let him win.

Bucky and Tick walked up to Ashley while he was sitting on the back of the truck. In Tick's left hand he carried, on a napkin, three different kinds of cake. Bucky was cracking ice from his cup of lemonade and rubbing his over-stuffed stomach. Ashley laughed when he saw the cake in Tick's hand.

"Man, where does all that food go?" he asked Tick, as the two friends sat down on the back of the truck beside him.

Tick offered him the piece of caramel cake. "Man, I couldn't eat another bite if my life depended on it," Ashley said.

The three of them sat talking and swinging their feet, looking out at the people standing in groups of three or four, some walking about greeting old friends, some still eating.

Ben Pickins walked toward them, his guitar under his arm.

Ben was skinnier than Tick and, of all the guitar players in Mason County, and there were quite a few, Ben could outpick them all. And whenever and wherever he stopped, if he had his guitar strapped around his neck, a crowd gathered and requested their favorite pieces.

Ben hadn't been at the truck more than two minutes before people began to come from all directions. Soon the truck was surrounded by about forty or fifty people, all eyes upon the gray-headed man with long magic fingers.

Ben looked around at the people and smiled.

Someone pushed a stool toward him and he slid off the back of the truck and onto the stool. He stroked the guitar gently, and then his fingers began to run wild. A loud applause rose from the crowd and the requests began to roll in.

"Hey, Ben, how 'bout 'Mama, Shake That Thing?'" a half-drunken man yelled, and Fannle Mae Johnson poked him in the ribs with her elbow to remind him that Reverend Edwards was present.

"Play 'Going Down the Road Feeling Bad,' Ben," someone yelled, and the crowd cheered. It was a favorite of just about everybody. Ben lowered his head and closed his eyes, and the shrill sounds of his guitar music could be heard all the way down to the pond. Ben could make that old guitar talk.

He ended with an old hymn and everyone joined in singing, "Just a Closer Walk with Thee." Then, with the leftover food packed in the cars and trucks and wagons, they all said their good-byes, and the line of vehicles moved toward the old Sandy Fork Road.

Ashley pulled the pickup out on the main road. Bessie sat between him and Stoner, and Minnie and Eva sat behind with the food, as they had done coming to the picnic.

Bessie was still softly humming "Just a Closer Walk with Thee." She stopped humming and said, "It was nice, wasn't it?" She had a smile on her face as she looked straight ahead at the road meeting them.

Ashley pressed on the accelerator. "Old Ben can really play."

Stoner said, "It's been one of the happiest days of my life. There may be some rough times ahead, but days like this make it all worthwhile."

Ashley glanced over at Stoner. He had never heard him sound so sentimental. He wondered if Stoner felt the same uneasiness that he himself felt. Thomas Rucker had been mighty quiet since leaving the courtroom that day, yelling that he would get even with Stoner Brooks, that no nigger was going to split his scalp open and get away with it.

Chapter 12

Mr. Brinkley had let Thomas Rucker go as overseer of his farms because too many good workers were leaving. And because of Rucker's quick temper and known prejudice towards blacks, other planters were refusing to hire him.

Remembering what he once had, Rucker began to drink heavily and hang out with some redneck bigots who were said to be members of the Ku Klux Klan. By the first of the year Rucker was living as poorly as the poorest tenant farmer, living with his wife and daughter in a small house, farming a few acres of land. His house was located across the highway from Snellings's general store, up a long, winding path, directly across the field from Mary Jo's best friend, Sue Ellen Baines.

Since the day of Stoner Brooks's trial, when the

court had set him free, Rucker believed that the trend of punishment of blacks had been broken and that the whites of Mason County needed their own method for punishing blacks who stepped out of line. So Rucker and these men had formed a group called the "Protectors," of which Rucker was leader.

Stoner Brooks had moved his family into the little house on Peterson's farm. The white five-room house with running water sat on a hill covered with green grass.

Things seemed to be going pretty smoothly for Stoner, but Ashley was uneasy. He had heard through the grapevine about the Protectors, that they had said Stoner Brooks was living too well for a nigger who had split open a white man's head, and if the law wouldn't punish him they would.

Ashley tried to ignore this rumor, but it had begun to weigh on his mind as heavily as the trial, and wherever he went now there was talk of the Protectors. And that past Sunday morning they had found a black farmer named Ernest Tatum lying by the roadside unconscious, with two broken arms.

Ernest had four pretty daughters, whom he guarded like precious jewels. His oldest, Jean, had gone up to the Big House where they lived one evening to get a pail of milk from the barn. The white overseer had caught Jean alone in the barn and beaten her. Ernest had gone straight up there and beaten the overseer badly. The rumor was that the Protectors had caught Ernest alone on his way from work that Saturday night and punished him.

Ashley had done everything in his power to keep this latest development from Stoner, which was possible only because Stoner worked all day and seldom went anyplace, and didn't even know about the Protectors.

Ashley and Stoner had taken a load of wood to Jenkins's wood yard in town late that Saturday evening. Before they could finish unloading the wood, a violent storm had come, uprooting trees and lifting off housetops. It had lasted far into the night, preventing Ashley and Stoner from going home. Ashley had suggested to Stoner that they spend the night in town, but Stoner wouldn't hear of it. So now Ashley and Stoner were heading home at two o'clock in the morning, on the lonely highway.

Ashley glared at the shiny black road ahead, wishing he had told Stoner the whole story of the Protectors, so he wouldn't have insisted on coming home so late at night when few people were out on the roads.

Ashley had noticed headlights in his rearview mirror for some time now and was getting nervous. He looked over at Stoner. "You 'sleep?"

Stoner, his head lying to the side, quickly straightened. "I nodded off a little bit there," he said, rubbing his eyes. Then he turned and looked back at the headlights behind them but said nothing.

The car kept getting closer and closer and Ashley slowed down to let it pass, but it wouldn't; it just kept on their tail, its headlights glaring into Ashley's rearview mirror and almost blinding him.

"What's that car trying to do?" Stoner asked

sharply.

"I don't know, Daddy, but I ain't stopping for nothing," Ashley said, gripping the steering wheel in anticipation of trouble, while Stoner sat turned around in his seat watching the car.

Suddenly the car on their tail lunged forward and gave the truck a hard bump, throwing Ashley and Stoner almost through the windshield.

"What in the...? Somebody's trying to run us off the road!" Stoner yelled angrily. Ashley said nothing, only braced himself in the seat, gripping the steering wheel and pressing the gas pedal all the way down to the floorboard.

The next violent thrust sent the truck careening out of control across the rain-slicked road, where it plunged into the ditch, the wheels continuing to spin in the soft earth.

Ashley and Stoner looked back. The car had pulled onto the shoulder and the lights had been turned off. Over the sound of the struggling engine as Ashley tried to work the truck out of the ditch, he yelled to Stoner to lock his door. He finally gave up trying to start the truck and began to search around for some sort of weapon; there was nothing but an old rag and a windshield wiper.

As Stoner struggled to make the broken lock on his door work, he realized someone was trying to yank the door open. He grabbed the door handle and pulled on it, but the door was wrenched from his grip.

By the moonlight Ashley and Stoner could see there were four men wearing white hoods, the black eyeholes glaring at them. The silence was terrifying!

Stoner was pulled from the truck by two of the men and dragged toward the cornfield. Stoner, being a big strong man, put up a terrific fight, but they got the better of him and dragged him into the cornfield.

Ashley lunged from the truck to try to help Stoner, but he was immediately seized and his arms pinned behind him. He fought wildly, cursing and telling them he knew who they were. Then he heard Stoner cry out in pain.

The truck sat stuck in the ditch, its lights glaring, and far up the road the lights of an oncoming car pierced the blackness.

Just then the two big men ran out of the cornfield and one said to the two struggling with Ashley, "Come on. Let's get out of here. Somebody's coming!"

The four men ran and jumped in their car and it sped off up the road, its tires screeching against the macadam.

Ashley groped through the darkness, looking for Stoner and calling him. He heard a low, mournful cry. By the time he reached him Stoner had passed out, lying face down in the dirt like a dead man.

When the two black men in the approaching car saw the lights glaring from the ditch, they pulled over and stopped. By now Ashley had brought Stoner and laid him on the ground where he could see him by the truck lights.

"What in the hell is going on here?" one of the black men yelled, running toward Ashley, who was bending over Stoner, calling him and wiping dirt from his face and nostrils.

Ashley looked up at Nate and Joe Cotton, two

brothers who worked on Peterson's farm.

"Help me, man," Ashley said. "They've hurt Daddy bad. Talk to me, Daddy," Ashley kept saying, his voice cracking with emotion.

Stoner suddenly opened his eyes and cried out with pain, pointing to his ankle.

"Help me get him to the hospital, man," Ashley said to Joe, and they laid Stoner on the backseat of Joe's car and Ashley got behind with him. Nate and Joe got in front and the car sped off down the road toward the hospital.

"It's broke, Ashley," Stoner said between moans. The pain in his ankle was excruciating and he couldn't move his leg. "They've messed up my ankle, the sons of bitches! They stomped on it!"

Joe listened to Ashley tell what happened, then he said there was a group of black men, led by a man named Willie Green, who went around getting even with whites who mistreated blacks.

Willie Green had served two years behind bars for beating a white man who had raped his wife. He had vowed that when he was set free he would take the law into his own hands, because he sincerely believed this was the only way the black man could have justice.

Ashley paced back and forth in the colored section of the emergency room at Mason Hospital, wondering what his mother must be going through, not knowing what had happened to them. He hadn't seen or heard from Stoner since they wheeled him through a door and cautioned Ashley to stay out.

In the emergency room blacks sat in little wood

chairs lined against the wall, hollow eyes staring at closed doors, waiting and waiting and waiting.

The door opened and two men dressed in white brought in a black man on a stretcher, his white shirt soaked with blood. Ashley stood motionless, staring at the man's livid face as he was wheeled by him into a room where they left him. The man was already dead.

A doctor came out of one of the little rooms and walked over to a black woman. She dropped her face into her hands and began to cry like a baby.

There was a vacant seat, but Ashley could not bring himself to sit down; he continued to pace. He looked around as the door to the emergency room swung open again. Two men held up a third man between them, walking along holding his eyeball on his palm as he cupped his hand to his face; the eyeball was being held to the socket by a single string-like substance.

Ashley turned his head. The soft-drink machine sat in the lobby, and he wheeled around and went and bought a cold drink to calm his nerves. When he had almost finished, the door to the room where they had taken Stoner opened and a doctor walked out looking around.

The overweight doctor introduced himself as Dr. Wimberly. "Are you Mr. Brooks's son?"

"Yes, sir. How is my father?"

"He's resting now. But his ankle's busted up pretty bad. He'll have to wear a cast for a while."

Ashley stared at the doctor while he explained Stoner's condition, finally finding the words to say that Stoner might never walk straight again, that it would take a miracle.

In the months that followed Stoner's injury, Ashley did the work of two men, while Stoner hobbled around in a cast. Ashley's dream of starting college had to be put on hold.

Chapter 13

The Chicken Shack was crowded when Bucky and Tick got there that Saturday night. In the center of the dance floor skirts were flying high, and black and brown and yellow thighs were being eyed by men on the sidelines.

The loud, ear-splitting music rang out into the open fields for miles around. There were mixed scents of cheap perfume, Saturday night sweet soaps, Palmer's hair pomade, Spearmint and Juicy Fruit gum, and Lucky Strike and Camel cigarette smoke.

Joe was steadily wiping sweat from his forehead with the hem of his apron, while he popped caps on ice-cold sodas behind the counter.

Bucky and Tick walked up. Tick said, "Whatcha know, Joe?"

"Don't know nothing much," Joe said. "What about

yourself?"

"Ain't nothing shaking but the leaves on the trees," Tick said. "Gimme a grape."

Tick leaned back against the counter, sipping the soda and looking out at the dance floor. "There's old Stick spinning around out there," he said, laughing. "Lord, please don't let that girl's dress fly up," he said. "She's got the skinniest legs in Mason."

Joe grinned. "Boys say that thing of hers is good, though."

Just then Ashley walked in. It had been weeks since he had been to the Chicken Shack, but this particular Saturday night he felt the need of some fun and dancing.

"Ashley Brooks," Bucky yelled across the floor, and several girls turned to look. He smiled as he returned the wave of a girl dancing with her boyfriend.

Ashley walked over to where Bucky and Tick stood at the counter.

"I ain't seen you in a coon's age, man," Tick said to Ashley.

"It's been kinda rough with Daddy laid up," Ashley said.

"How's he doing?" Joe asked. "Is his ankle gonna be all right when they take the cast off?"

Ashley sighed. "I don't know. Doctors don't seem to have much hope of it."

"Doctors don't know nothing," Joe said. "They say you gonna die when you ain't, and you ain't gonna die when you is. I don't go to 'em if I can help it."

Joe changed the subject. "Who's that pretty long-haired girl standing over there with the yellow dress on?"

They all looked around. "Man, you know her. That's Daisy Lane that works at Slim's Cafe," Ashley said.

"Must be one of them sheltered girls," Joe said. "Don't see her here much."

Tick said, "If I had a daughter that pretty I'd shelter her too."

Daisy Lane was throwing furtive glances at Ashley. She had begged hard and it had paid off. Her parents had let her come to the Chicken Shack with her cousin Marie and her boyfriend. When Daisy had first walked in the place, she had immediately scanned the room hoping to see Ashley there. When she did not see him, she had been severely disappointed.

Then she had stood and watched the door until her eyes burned. And when Ashley finally walked in and those girls had waved to him she had wanted to scratch their eyes out. She felt that he was hers, and she his, even if he didn't know it yet, which was why she had refused every young man who had come up and asked her to dance.

A slow song came on and Daisy glanced over at the counter, where her eyes had kept Ashley captured. He was gone. It felt as if her heart dropped to the floor. *All that begging,* Daisy thought. *And all that I did to make myself pretty for him. He doesn't even know I exist.*

Out of the corner of her eye Daisy glimpsed a hand extended toward her. It was Ashley asking her to dance.

"Hi, Daisy," Ashley said. "You're looking mighty

beautiful tonight." When she took his hand, he led her to the middle of the dance floor by her fingertips, where he took her in his arms and they began to sway to the love song playing. "Take me in your arms and soothe my aching heart," the velvety voice of the lady singer cried.

"You come here often?" Ashley asked Daisy, the sweet fragrance of her talcum powder enveloping him.

"Not often. My parents won't let me come here alone," Daisy said.

"Who's the lucky guy?" Ashley asked, dancing smoothly.

"Huh? Oh! I came with my cousin Marie and her boyfriend," Daisy replied, happy to let Ashley know that no boy had brought her.

"I'm glad to know that," Ashley said, drawing her a bit closer.

She stepped on his foot. "Oh! I'm sorry!"

"That's all right," Ashley said. "My corn's on the other foot."

Daisy laughed again, feeling more at ease. Not only was Ashley Brooks good-looking, she thought, but he had a sense of humor and knew how to put a nervous girl at ease.

The second dance they got to know each other better, each asking the other questions about their background and their family.

By the third dance they were cheek to cheek. Three guys had come up and tapped Ashley on the shoulder, and he had ignored them. He was falling in love.

Since Leonard's death Rosa had been withdrawn; now

she was acting strangely. Bessie was concerned about her sister. Rosa had stayed inside for weeks now, refusing to leave the house, the shades drawn day and night. Each time Bessie sent Ashley to bring her over for dinner or a visit, Rosa would refuse, saying, "I'm all right. I'm here with Leonard."

One morning Ashley stopped by to check on Rosa before going to work and noticed that she was wearing a bandage on her wrist and the house smelled of rubbing alcohol. Rosa said she had cut her wrist while slicing meat, but Ashley didn't believe her.

The guilt that Rosa felt was devastating to her—guilt at having wished Leonard would die. In her own mind she had come to believe that Leonard's death had been her fault.

Rosa sat on the bed now, looking over at Leonard's pillow. She thought of the many nights he had suffered with severe headaches. If only she had gotten him to a doctor sooner, she thought, her eyes running full of tears. She started to cry and then she lay on the bed and began hugging Leonard's pillow.

When Rosa heard the knock on the door, she let go of the pillow and went to the door, cracked it, and peeped out. "I'm all right, Ashley," she said, peering through the crack.

Ashley pushed the door open and walked in. "Pack your clothes, Aunt Rosa. Ma said for me not to come back without you."

"I can't, Ashley," Rosa said, looking straight at him, a serious expression on her face. "I can't leave Leonard."

Ashley looked around the dark, eerie room, then

back at Rosa. After fifteen minutes of trying to convince her that he wouldn't leave without her, she gave in and went to pack.

Ashley waited in a chair beside the front door. It lay open, and bright sunshine streamed into the dark, musty-smelling house. Ashley knew something was terribly wrong with his aunt. She usually kept her house immaculately clean.

Ashley had given Rosa plenty of time to pack. He was about to get up and go check on her when he heard her talking as though someone was in the room with her.

He eased up from the chair and crept to the room and stopped just outside the door, looking in. A suitcase lay open on the bed and clothes—some of Leonard's as well as Rosa's—lay strewn all over the bed.

"He wants me to leave you here by yourself, Leonard. All of them want me to leave you." Rosa stopped packing and sat on the side of the bed, crying.

Ashley walked into the room. "It's all right, Aunt Rosa. Come on." He took her by the hand and led her out of the house. All the way to the truck Rosa kept looking back, telling Leonard to come on.

As Ashley drove out of Rosa's yard he peeped back over his shoulder to see if Leonard actually might be standing in the yard. He didn't want to believe in haunts, but he had grown up with that junk in his mind. When he had been in that dark house and Rosa had been talking to Leonard, the hair at the nape of Ashley's neck had stood on edge, and he had to tell himself that he wasn't afraid of ghosts.

The sky hung sad and still over the pickup truck that Monday afternoon as Ashley and Stoner headed home from the doctor. Stoner had just had his cast removed, and Ashley couldn't forget the doctor's heartbreaking announcement.

"Is this the way I got to walk the rest of my life?" Stoner had asked the doctor, after hobbling across the floor for the first time without the cast.

"I'm afraid so," the doctor said. That foot was in pretty bad shape, Stoner. You're lucky it healed as well as it has." The doctor scratched his head. "Of course there might be some bone specialist up north somewhere who could straighten out that ankle, but it would take a lot of money." He rubbed the back of his neck. "I'm really not sure it can be fixed."

As they drove toward home, Ashley glanced over at Stoner, who was sitting quietly beside him, clutching a bag of assorted candy for Eva. The gray at his temples seemed to have spread over his entire head within the last few months, Ashley thought. But he was taking the bad news well.

He knew Stoner was torn apart inside at the prospect of being a cripple the rest of his life. *What has he ever done to anybody to get this kind of punishment?* Ashley thought. *It just can't end this way. I'll find a doctor.* Ashley's eyes welled up with tears and he batted them back.

Ashley and his family had lived on Peterson's farm for a little over three months. Stoner, though deeply depressed at times over his crippled foot, was managing to tend the crops, and Bessie was working for Mrs. Peterson on the side, bringing in a little spending change.

Christmas had come and gone. Colleges everywhere would soon be signing up students for second semesters.

After supper that night, Ashley didn't wait for dessert. He walked out in the backyard and sat on a stump to let the cold wash over him while he did some serious thinking.

It was now or never, he told himself. There would always be something that would deter him from starting college if he stood back and did nothing. He needed to make some immediate plans.

"God," he muttered, "which way do I turn? What do I do first?"

Then, as if she were standing beside him, Ashley felt his grandmother's presence.

He glanced up at the sky. "Would I be wrong leaving here now, with Daddy hobbling around on that crippled foot, trying to do a day's work? Anyway, how can I get into college anywhere this late? And how can I come up with the money? I'm sure to need way more than I've saved."

Then it hit him: Mr. Taylor. Ashley had gone up to the lawyer to shake hands with him that day after the trial to thank him. Mr. Taylor had told Ashley then that, if there was any way he could help him in the future, just to let him know. Ashley liked the man a lot. Why hadn't he thought of him before?

And he was certain he could borrow some money

from Mr. Peterson if he needed to. He would pay him back every cent of it; he didn't want charity, nor did he want payback for saving the man's son.

All the time Ashley was making plans for college, something was bothering him—Daisy Lane. He and Daisy had been going together for almost two months. He didn't want to lose her.

Ashley got up and walked back inside the kitchen. It was warm and cozy there, with the delicious aroma of blueberry pie baking still hanging heavy in the air. His family was sitting around the table eating pie. He sat down on the bench with Minnie and Eva, propping his elbows on the table and lacing his fingers while Bessie cut him a piece of pie and placed it before him.

Ashley forked up a mouthful of pie, chewed it, and took a swallow of milk. He looked over at Stoner. "Daddy, what would you think of me starting to college soon? You think you could do without me?"

Stoner stopped his forkful of pie in mid-air. His eyes locked with Ashley's.

"It's the best thing you could ever do in your life," Stoner said. "Sho, I can get along without you."

Bessie held her composure for a brief moment, then her joy came pouring out. "Ashley. Oh, Ashley. Lord..., do you think? Lord, I'd be the happiest person in the whole world!"

"What about the money?" Stoner asked. "Will you have enough?"

"If I don't, I can get some from Mr. Peterson." ·

"Where will you go?" Stoner asked.

"St. Augustine's in Raleigh. That's the one I've

been thinking about."

"It ain't too late to get in? It's the middle of the year."

"I can start the second semester. Second semester begins soon."

"You can get in just like that?"

Ashley stared at the worn spot on the tablecloth. "I'll see if Mr. Taylor will put in a good word for me. You heard what he said that day at the trial."

Eva sat listening, batting her eyes anxiously. "How long do it take to be a lawyer, Ashley?"

"Long time," Ashley said.

"How far is Raleigh?" Minnie asked, turning to face Ashley on the bench.

"Pretty long ways."

Bessie squeezed her palms together. "Our son going to college! Do you know how good that makes me feel?" she said to no one in particular. "This calls for a celebration!"

With that Bessie got up from the table and cut everybody another slice of pie. "Our Ashley," she said proudly. "Going to college!"

Chapter 14

Daisy Lane had cleaned the coffee pot that Saturday morning at Slim's Cafe and made fresh coffee. She poured herself a bubbling cupful and was bringing the cup to her lips when she heard the front door open. She looked around to see who had come in. The color drained from her lips and her heart began to race wildly. Tom Willis, disheveled and red-eyed, was striding through the cafe toward the counter, his eyes arrogantly appraising her body.

Clyde, the cook, had told Daisy about the rumor that Tom Willis was going around telling people that Daisy was his girl and he intended to kill anybody who messed with her.

Daisy knew that Tom Willis was telling this outright lie because of the feud he had going on with Ashley. But still she was afraid of him and wanted to go to the back of the cafe and stay there till he was gone. But she couldn't. The usual breakfast crowd was beginning to arrive.

Tom Willis sat—loomed—on the stool sipping black coffee and eyeing Daisy until after the crowd cleared out at ten o'clock. Daisy had rattled cups and saucers, dropped spoons and forks, and given three people the wrong change.

Soon, Tom Willis was the only customer left in the cafe, and Daisy's stomach began to churn, because it was almost time for Clyde to go get the barbecue for the lunch crowd.

Clyde looked at Daisy. "You gonna be all right? Daisy nodded. Clyde was taking off his long white apron and watching Tom out of the corner of his eye. "I'll be back in a minute," Clyde said for Tom's benefit; Daisy knew it would take Clyde at least thirty minutes to walk to get the barbecue, since he weighed nearly three hundred pounds.

After watching Clyde disappear up the street, Daisy turned, avoiding Tom's eyes, and walked over to the drink box to begin putting in drinks, hoping someone would walk in soon.

"You trying to ignore me?" asked Tom Willis, his voice sounding like little pebbles hitting against one another. Daisy didn't answer, nor did she look back at Tom. "I finally got you all to myself, little mama. Whatcha think of that?" There was a long silence. "Come over here!" Tom demanded. "I want to order something."

Daisy rolled her eyes at him, then walked over and stood before him behind the counter, at what she hoped was a safe distance, her knees trembling. He didn't order anything, only looked her up and down, his red eyes stopping on her hips.

"What do you want to order?" Daisy asked sharply.

"Just what you see me looking at," Tom said, his eyes glued to the bottom part of her body. Tom grinned. "We could lock the door and go in the back and have a little fun."

Daisy remembered the pistol Slim kept in back of the cash register. She would blow his head off if he put his hands on her, she thought. She began to ease toward the cash register.

"Where the hell you going, woman? Come on back over here. I want to ask you a question."

Daisy walked back cautiously.

"What time do you get off work tonight?

"My daddy picks me up every night," Daisy said sharply, rolling her eyes at him.

"What daddy? You talking 'bout that Ashley Brooks—that goddamned, motherfucking Ashley Brooks?"

Daisy stared into his angry eyes. He was getting angrier by the minute. She didn't want to shoot any-one, had never held a gun in her hand in her life. She thought of running out the door.

Tom Willis leaned on the counter, pointing a fin-ger at Daisy. "You just remember this, little mama. You can just forget about that motherfucking Ashley, because I'm gonna fix his ass!" He drained his cof-fee cup, took out a dollar, and waved at her.

Daisy hesitated to move out of her tracks. Then she walked over and reached for the dollar to give him his change.

He grabbed her wrist, but she managed to pull away, snatching it from his big strong hand. He jumped off the stool, wide-eyed, and started behind the counter. Daisy ran toward the cash register just as two burly customers walked in.

The men stopped in their tracks, watching Tom Willis behind the counter. Tom walked back around the counter and hurried out of the cafe.

Mae and Annie Willis were sisters-in-law. Mae was Leon Willis's mother, and Annie was the mother of the three "Willis boys."

Mae could stand on her back porch and see the chimney of Annie's house. They had worn a path through the cornfield visiting each other, talking of their ailments, canning, making bed quilts. They also discussed Annie's mean sons, and sometimes they talked about Leon and his white girlfriend, Mary Jo Rucker.

Annie was visiting Mae that evening. She was standing at the window looking out at the rain coming down, feeling sorry for herself. It hadn't been easy, trying to raise three boys alone. Their father had been stabbed to death in a fight one Saturday at a dance hall when the boys were very young. He had been abusive to his sons and they were glad when he died.

Annie turned to Mae, who was sitting in the kitchen, churning. "Every time I look up, Tom's in trouble with the law," she said. "I don't know what's wrong with that boy. Sometimes I wonder if his mind's all right." She sighed. "I guess he just takes after his daddy. Ben stayed in trouble till the day somebody killed him." Annie picked up a syrupy sweet potato from a batch Mae had in a pan on the stove, still warm from the oven. She peeled it, took a big bite out of it, and chewed it up. "They're out of my hands now; they're grown men. I'll just leave them to the law."

Mae checked the churn; the butter had come, a golden ball swimming on top of the buttermilk inside the old hand churn. Raising Leon alone hadn't been any easier. Years ago, Leon's father had run off with some woman without any warning—just up and left one day—when Leon was a baby. Mae hadn't heard a word from him since. She didn't know if he was alive or dead.

But Mae knew that there was no comparison between Leon and Annie's boys; Leon didn't have a mean bone in his body. Annie would be the first to agree with her.

Annie changed the subject. "How are Leon and his white girlfriend getting along?" she asked Mae.

"Mary Jo's a nice girl," Mae said. "She seems to think a lot of Leon."

Annie chuckled. "I'll bet old Thomas Rucker would drop dead in his tracks if he knowed his daughter was going with a nigger."

"Probably would," Mae said, "as much as he loves that girl. He hates the ground a nigger walks on, but they say Mary Jo's his heart." Mae grew silent, staring thoughtfully at the floor. "I hope to God Thomas Rucker don't find out about Leon and Mary Jo. No telling what he might do to Leon."

There was a long silence; then Annie said, "I hope nothing happens to Leon, but it serves him right whatever happens to him. What makes him want to go running after white women as many black women as there is in the world?"

"I'm worried sick, Annie," May said. "Every time Leon goes out of this house I don't know if I'll ever see him alive again."

That night Leon and Mary Jo went riding. They always came back as late as possible, hoping to avoid anyone seeing them.

Mary Joe jumped out of the car and ran across the road and up the long, winding path home.

After sitting and watching her safely out of sight, Leon drove off. When he passed Snellings's store, something shiny behind the store caught his eye. He stopped the car abruptly and eased back to get a good look, his headlights off. Sure enough, there sat a car parked behind the store, where no car ever parked. Leon was scared. He suspected it was some white man who had been watching him and Mary Jo. He liked Mary Jo a lot. They had fun together, but she was not worth getting lynched for, he thought.

It was almost time for the new semester to start at the college. Ashley was excited about the prospect of leaving, but he was also sad about leaving his family and friends, especially Daisy Lane. Ashley pressed on the accelerator and watched the little red needle go almost to fifty before it stopped and began to shimmy. He had driven the old truck so long it seemed like a good friend. He glanced at his red cap on the dashboard. It had become a part of him too. *People probably wouldn't recognize me without it*, he thought.

Ashley was on his way to town that Saturday evening around sunset. He and Daisy had a date after Daisy got off work at the cafe. It was to be their last night together before Ashley left for college.

Things had worked out just as Ashley had hoped. It happened that Moses Taylor was a good friend of the president of St. Augustine's College. On his next trip to Raleigh, Mr. Taylor got the application forms and put in a good word for Ashley. After doing all the paperwork, Ashley had quickly mailed the forms to the college. And Mr. Peterson had loaned Ashley more money than he probably would need; he wanted it to be a gift to Ashley, but Ashley would only accept it as a loan.

Except for the tires whining against the highway, it was quiet in the truck as Ashley watched the road rushing to meet him. He felt strangely. It was kind of a sad and lonely feeling. The wind coming through the crack over the window glass seemed to be whispering something to him. He had never felt this way before. *You're in love, nigger*, he thought, smiling to himself. *Your ass would have to go fall in love just when you're ready to leave.*

Later, when Ashley and Daisy were leaving the cafe, walking toward the truck parked up the street, Ashley suddenly stopped.

"What is it?" Daisy asked.

"I thought I saw somebody getting out of my truck," Ashley said.

"Did you lock the doors?"

"Ain't nothing in there nobody would want," Ashley said, peering through the darkness toward the truck. Now he could see no one; if there had been someone in the truck, he had disappeared into the darkness.

They walked on.

At the movie, Daisy could hardly see the picture on the screen for the tears that welled up in her eyes.

"Oh, Ashley," she said. "I don't want you to leave."

Sitting with his arm around her, he pulled her to him and kissed her. "It's not like I'm going away forever," he said. "I'll be coming back whenever I can."

Oddly enough, the movie was about a young man's last night out with his girl before going off to war. The characters looked sad, the music was sad, and Daisy was certainly sad. Toward the end of the movie the young man was killed at war, and when the girl was told she buried her face in her hands and burst into tears. Daisy cried, too.

Ashley took Daisy straight home after the movie, but they parked the truck in front of her house, sitting and talking for almost two hours, saying their good-byes. Then Ashley drove by the Chicken Shack to say good-bye to the fellas.

Robert Stover was there. "So you're leaving tomorrow?" he asked.

"Yeah, Ashley replied. "I planned to stop by your house if you weren't here." He looked Robert over from his long sideburns to his keen-toed shoes. "Looks like you're all healed up."

"I am," Robert said. "I finally realized that white

lightning was killing me and I'm leaving it alone. I feel like a new person."

"Yeah," Ashley said. "Keep on leaving it alone."

Robert grinned. "Hey, you gonna leave that pretty woman of yours here for the wolves to get?"

Ashley looked at him and didn't answer.

"You want me to take care of her while you gone?" he asked jokingly.

Ashley narrowed his eyes and pointed a finger at Robert. "Go near her, asshole motherfucker, and I'll break your head!"

They laughed and joked and messed around for a while and Ashley went home.

That same night Leon picked up Mary Jo and took her home with him for dinner.

For dessert Mae had made a pan of rich, spicy gingerbread, Mary Jo's favorite. Mary Jo asked Leon if he remembered the day she had taken him a piece down to the barn when he was whitewashing the walls and he had stood eating it with whitewash all over his hands. Leon remembered and told her he had been so scared her father was going to catch them together that he hardly knew what the hell he was doing.

Mae commented to Leon, "Your cousins Tank and Lewis said they was coming over to play some cards with you tonight."

Leon looked at Mary Jo and said, "We'd better go before they get here." He didn't want to be bothered with the likes of them making eyes at Mary Jo and using their foul language.

Sometimes Leon could tolerate Tank and Lewis if

they hadn't been drinking, but Tom was another story.
Leon thought the man was *off.*

By the time Tank and Lewis, both half drunk, got
to Mae's house that night, Leon and Mary Jo had gone
for their drive and Leon had taken her home, then
gone on alone to the Chicken Shack.

Tank and Lewis were disappointed to find that Leon
wasn't home, but they stayed and talked to their aunt
for about fifteen minutes. When they were ready to
leave Mae said, "Wait a minute; take your mama this
jar of peach preserves I promised her." Mae left them
standing at the door and came back, wiping off the
jar of preserves with the sleeve of her nightgown.

"Where's that brother of yours?" she asked them.
Before one of them could answer she added, "Y'all
ought not to do your poor old mama like you do. That
brother of yours is gonna be the death of her yet; you
just watch and see. Where is he tonight, out fighting
somewhere?"

"No'm," Tank said. "Tom's home. He came home
acting strange tonight. Didn't eat supper. Went straight
to bed."

Leon had had an uneasy feeling in his gut ever
since the night he had seen that car parked behind the
store when he had taken Mary Jo home. When Leon
took Mary Jo home that night, a storm was brewing
and the sky was purplish black, the strong wind whip-
ping and lashing dried cornstalks in the field. They
sat together in the car, checking around before Mary
Jo got out. Then, when it looked safe enough, she
jumped out and trotted across the road and up the path.

Leon sat and watched her through the car window until she was out of sight up the path, then waited a few more minutes to give her time to get into her house.

On his way home, Leon stopped by the Chicken Shack.

Just as Mary Jo approached the first of the three tobacco barns along the path, she began to run, aware that she was out of Leon's sight. When it started raining she ran a little faster, the cold rain beating her in the face. Approaching the second barn she sensed someone behind her.

She turned to look but didn't have a chance to see who it was. The person suddenly grabbed her and clamped a hand over her mouth and eyes. She tried to scream but only managed to make muffled noises. The man dragged her inside the pitch-dark barn and threw her down on the sandy floor. She fought him till she had no strength left, but he was too strong for her, managing to pin her down and rip off her clothing.

When she felt his hot breath close to her face she dug her fingernails into his flesh. He struck her jaw with his fist, and she blacked out.

In pain and aware that she had been raped, Mary Jo drifted back into consciousness to the sound of a loud clap of thunder. For a moment she lay there, afraid her attacker was still somewhere around. Then slowly and guardedly she got to her feet, listening for sounds in the barn. She heard only hard rain beating against the tin roof of the barn.

With a sharp pain in her groin and her head aching

from the blow she had been given, she pulled her
clothing on as best she could and groped her way to
the barn door. Whimpering softly like a wounded ani-
mal she stood there, her eyes searching the darkness.
When she was sure there was no one about, she scur-
ried out of the barn and ran wildly up the path home.

Chapter 15

Thomas Rucker had sobered up. He had been drunk ever since that morning when he and Alice had a big argument over Mary Jo and he had belted his wife. She had turned and glared at him, her nose red as a beet from crying and her eyes puffy, saying nothing, just glaring at him for a long time. Then, the minute her daughter left the house, she left too. For good.

"Fuck her!" Rucker said, slumped in an armchair in the living room, listening to the rain beating against the window. "Let her go where the fuck she wants to. All she cared about was my money anyhow. His face brightened as he thought of his daughter. *She's all I got left*, he thought, sighing self-pityingly. *The niggers have caused me to lose everything. Everything. Even my pride.... When they'll let a nigger go free after he's split open a white man's head..., man can't hold up his head. He feels less than shit!*

Realizing suddenly that it was eleven-thirty, Rucker began to worry about his daughter. Why wasn't she home by now? After Mary Jo had gone out, saying she was meeting Sue Ellen to go to a movie, Alice had packed and gone to stay at her sister's. Had Mary Jo somehow learned that her mother had left and had gone to stay with her? Maybe she didn't want to come home; maybe she was staying at Sue Ellen's.

Rucker straightened in the chair and listened. He thought he heard a strange noise. "Traipsing up and down the road at night," Rucker muttered. "Any god-damned thing could happen to her!"

Their final argument had been about Mary Jo traipsing up and down the road. Alice blamed him. "She doesn't have a decent home to come to anymore. We fuss and fight all the time," she had said. "She hates you for hating the blacks so much."

Rucker shifted position in the chair and sat staring at the lapping flames in the fireplace, thinking of how it used to be. "Fucking black no-good lazy bastards!" he said, breathing heavily, his lips pursed and his eyes glaring into the red flames.

The banging on the door snapped Rucker out of his fit of anger, and he rose and hurried toward the front door, thinking it was about time his daughter finally got home.

Rucker unbolted the door and pulled it open. When he saw his daughter, his jaw dropped and his eyes widened. Mary Jo stood in the door with her hair plastered to her face, her clothes torn and disheveled, crying hysterically.

Sheriff Wendy and three of his deputies came to the Rucker home and began to comb the entire area around where Mary Jo was raped, while Rucker stormed through the house waving his fist in the air, talking of lynching.

Suddenly a deputy came running up to Sheriff Wendy, out of breath, waving something in his hand. "Found it in the barn," he said. "The nigger probably lost it in the dark before he ran out." In his hand was a red cap.

Rucker suddenly became very quiet. Then, staring at the cap, his voice trembling, he said, "Whoever the nigger is that this cap belongs to can kiss this old world good-bye, because when I get my hands on him he's a dead man! A fucking dead man!"

Rucker kept turning the cap over and over, examining every inch of it, until the sheriff reached out and took it from him.

"Now, Thomas," he said. "Take it easy. We don't know if it was a nigger that raped your girl. We don't know who this cap belongs to. But there's somebody I bet can tell us."

On Sunday morning when Snellings drove up to his store the sheriff's car was parked in front under the tree. Sheriff Wendy stayed outside while Snellings waited on his usual crowd of Sunday morning customers. The sheriff eyed every black man who went in the store. When the last customer left Sheriff Wendy got out and went in and told Snellings what had happened. He pulled the red cap from his back pocket. Snellings's mouth flew open, and he stood there staring disbelievingly at it.

"You recognize it, don't you?" the sheriff said. "I knew you would. Every nigger in Mason County comes in here. Tell me who it belongs to!"

When Snellings managed to recover from his surprise, he took a deep breath. He had seen Ashley Brooks wearing that cap more times than he could count. He remembered the morning Ashley had forgotten and left the cap at the store. He had come in and bought a grape drink, laying the cap on the counter while he stood drinking the drink and talking to him. Ashley had walked out and forgot his cap. Snellings had put it away to hold it for him until he came in again.

Ashley Brooks is no rapist, Snellings thought. *I'd bet my life on that.*

"Now come on, Tom," the sheriff said, clutching the butt of a cigar between the thumb and forefinger of his fat hand. "Don't be a fool. I know you know who it belongs to because your eyes popped out of your head when you first saw it."

Snellings did not reply but merely stood there shaking his head.

Sheriff Wendy drew hard on the cigar, tilted his head backwards, and forced the smoke up toward the ceiling. "Tom, Tom, Tom," he said, shaking his head. "I can see right now that you're gonna act like a fool about this. What's a nigger ever done for you except steal from you?"

Sheriff Wendy waited, drumming his fingers on the counter.

Snellings had started to sweat over his top lip. He wiped it off with the back of his hand. "I have no idea who that cap belongs to, Sheriff."

The sheriff chuckled a low, scornful laugh that made Snellings glance around at him. "Now, Tom, you wouldn't want me to do anything about that moonshine you been selling on the side, would you?"

Snellings looked at the sheriff, then dropped his eyes.

"I could close you down just like that." Sheriff Wendy snapped his fingers.

Wendy was sure that Snellings was protecting someone, and it angered him. He began to pace the floor, trying to decide how to make him talk, then wheeled around and walked back up to him. "OK, Tom," he said, a finger pointed at Snellings's nose, "I'll give you a few more hours to prod your memory. When I come back here this evening you'd better have a name for me, if you know what's good for you!"

He followed his protruding stomach out of the door.

As far back as Stoner Brooks could remember there had not been a brother or sister, an uncle or a cousin, or a grandmother or grandfather who had ever been inside a college door, much less attended one as a student. Now his son was leaving for college in a few hours, on the five o'clock bus.

They all sat at the table, having their last meal with Ashley for probably a long time. Bessie stood over Ashley's plate with a bowl of turnip greens, his favorite, heaping them on his plate for the second time.

Stoner washed down a mouthful of food with a big swallow of buttermilk. "You study hard, Ashley. You can be anything you wanna be. You just got to wanna be it bad enough."

Minnie narrowed her eyes in thought. "Daddy, can we go up to Raleigh and see Ashley sometimes?"

Bessie cut in, "Honey, Ashley'll be coming back home to visit from time to time. Won't you, Ashley?"

Ashley shoved the forkful of turnip greens in his mouth and bit down on the piece of crispy cornbread, nodding his head and chewing. "Every chance I get." He looked over at Stoner. "Daddy, you sure you can handle things OK without me?"

Stoner looked straight at Ashley. "Now what did I tell you? Don't you be going off worrying 'bout us. We'll be just fine. When Mr. Peterson opens that store and lets me run it, I won't have to worry 'bout nothing."

"He was talking to me about that this morning," Ashley said. "He talked like it won't be long either. I sure will be glad when you can stand behind the counter and wait on folks and won't have to go out in the bad weather."

Ashley grew quiet, remembering that morning over at Peterson's. The man had seemed so much like his own father. "You go on to college and study hard, son. You can be anything in this world you want to be," Peterson had said after opening his wallet and handing Ashley the money. Then he spat tobacco juice and held out his hand, giving Ashley a firm handshake.

Then Ashley had walked on out to the old green

pickup parked out by the mule stable and stood looking at it. He reached in to get his cap. It was nowhere
to be seen. He searched the truck over and over but
couldn't find it. *Wind probably blew it out the window,* he thought, and scoured the truck for it one more
time.

After dinner the Brooks family gathered in the living room, cherishing the last few hours together. It
was warm and cozy, a fire glowing in the fireplace.
Ashley's two suitcases sat by the front door, packed
and ready to go. Ashley stood with his elbow on the
fireplace mantel, talking to Bessie and Minnie and
Eva. Stoner was looking out the window.

"Somebody's coming," Stoner said.

Ashley went over and looked out. "That's Mr.
Snellings," he said. "Wonder what he's come up here
for."

"Seems to be in a mighty big hurry," Stoner said,
watching as Snellings got out of the car and came
rushing toward the house looking very upset.

Ashley opened the door. "Hello, Mr. Snellings," he
said, a quizzical expression on his face.

"Howdy, Ashley," Snellings said, walking in.
"Bessie. Stoner." He reached up and lifted his old felt
hat from his head and stood holding it in his hand,
looking anxiously at the floor for a moment before
finally turning to Ashley and saying, "Something terrible has happened!"

"What?"

"Last night Thomas Rucker's daughter was raped
in one of the tobacco barns on her way home!"

Ashley stared at Snellings, thinking, *Uh! That's*

"And they found your cap in the barn where she was raped," Snellings said.

Ashley glared at Snellings, as stunned as if he had been hit over the head with a two-by-four. "Found *my* cap? It couldn't have been mine!"

Snellings pinched the crease in the top of his hat. "It was yours, Ashley," he said in a low, even tone. "I'd recognize that cap of yours anywhere. And somebody else is bound to recognize it too. The sheriff was at the store waiting for me when I got there this morning. Had the cap with him. Kept waving it in my face. Said he knowed I knowed who it belonged to 'cause of the way I acted when he pulled it out and showed it to me." He looked at Ashley. "I was so stunned when I saw it was your cap I guess my mouth flew open."

Ashley walked over to the window and looked out, trying to think. Then it struck him—that night when he and Daisy were leaving the cafe, walking toward the truck, and he thought he had seen someone getting out of the truck. *Somebody deliberately took my cap then,* he thought, *planning to rape that girl and leave my cap to make it look like I did it.*

Ashley explained to everyone what had happened. "It's obvious somebody's trying to frame me!"

Snellings looked up at Ashley. "The sheriff's threatening me, Ashley. Says if I don't have a name for him by this afternoon he's gonna shut my store down. And he can do it because of the moonshine I sell. I'm gonna have to tell him. Too many people saw your cap at the store before you came back to get it. Too many people know you're the only one around with a cap like that."

They all stared at Snellings, knowing he was right. He was already risking a lot to delay the sheriff long enough to warn Ashley.

"I don't know how the hell your cap got in that barn, Ashley. But I do know one thing: you ain't no rapist." Snellings added.

Ashley paced the floor, nervously rubbing his palms together, thinking. He suddenly turned to Stoner and Bessie. "I've got to get away from here right now! For all we know somebody else has already identified my cap and the sheriff could be on his way to arrest me."

"Lord, Ashley!" Bessie cried. You can't leave! You've got to stay and straighten out this mess. Go to 'em and tell 'em what you told us. Tell 'em...."

"Bessie!" Stoner cut in sharply. "Them white folks ain't never going to believe Ashley didn't rape that girl! They won't even give him a chance of a courtroom trial. Let him go."

Ashley was still pacing the floor when Mr. Snellings hurried out to his car and sped off, afraid the sheriff would catch him there and figure out he was warning Ashley.

Down at Snellings's store the afternoon bus had been detained so that Sheriff Wendy and his deputies could check every passenger on it. The store yard was swarming with inquisitive spectators, black and white, since the word about the rape had spread. They watched the law officers going about their business

and stood around the yard—in separate groups, black
and white—conjecturing about the outcome.

When Sheriff Wendy showed the red cap to the reg-
ulars, asking if anybody could identify it, several
white men stepped forward to state unequivocably that
it belonged to Ashley Brooks.

When the sheriff was satisfied that Ashley Brooks
was not on the bus he released it. Then he got in his
car and headed out to where the Brookses lived.

Chapter 16

Stoner stared at Ashley. "Are you crazy? You can't stay there. Too many folks hang around that place!"

"Don't you see, Daddy," Ashley said. "That's the best place in the world to hide; the law never goes there."

Stoner gave him a long look.

"Oh, yeah," Ashley said, "they know all about what goes on there. That's where they get *their* supply of whiskey. They send for it, though. They wouldn't be caught dead in the place. Robert told me all about it. You see, if they ever went there they would have to admit they know what's going on and close Hattie down. So, by staying away, they can pretend they don't know what's happening."

Stoner and Bessie locked eyes. "I don't know," Stoner said. "I just hope they hurry and find out who did it soon, so you can stop running and hiding."

"I'll be all right," Ashley said. Robert offered to help me out with money for college. He won't mind putting me up till this mess is over. I'll hide out there and be one of Hattie's drunks for a while."

Eva giggled, then Minnie, too.

Mae and Annie Willis had been good friends for a long time. Now something was puzzling Mae; she couldn't get it out of her mind the peculiar way Annie had acted that day she stopped by Annie's house after Thomas Rucker's daughter, her son's girlfriend, had been raped.

This had been days ago. And now Annie had taken ill. Annie's son Tank had come banging on Mae's door late that Saturday afternoon, asking Mae if she would come see about his mother.

When Mae got to Annie's house, Annie lay in bed shivering so hard she could hardly speak, as if she were about to have a nervous breakdown. Mae finally managed to get Annie settled down, after making her a pot of herbal tea, and Annie fell asleep.

Mae had promised Annie she would sit with her for a while. And while Mae sat there she kept wondering why Annie's sons were avoiding her, all three of them staying in their room in the back of Annie's house.

Then Annie woke feeling much better. And Mae brought up the rape incident again, only Annie wouldn't talk about it, kept changing the subject.

Mae said good-bye to Annie and left. She wanted to get home through the cornfield before dark. After

Mae had walked a short distance she realized she had left her purse in Annie's house, so she turned around and went back. Pushing open Annie's front door, she ran smack into Tom Willis hurrying through the front room to the kitchen. It wasn't until Mae got home that she began to wonder about the scratches on Tom's face.

That night after Leon got home, Mae was afraid to mention what she had seen. She was afraid Leon would put two and two together, as she had done, and run right over to Annie's house and beat Tom Willis within an inch of his life for raping his girl. Mae knew Leon was no murderer, but she had been afraid he might become one if he ever found out who had attacked Mary Jo.

Mae wondered if she was the only one besides Tom's family who had seen the scratches. Each time she thought of Ashley Brooks having to leave home running like a common criminal, as nice a boy as he was, and that Tom Willis hiding out at home all that time, the real rapist, she got mad as hell. Mae was ready to go to the authorities and tell what she suspected, except she began to worry about her own safety. What if she *was* the only one who knew about the scars on Tom's face, other than his family? Perhaps Tom was watching every move she made!

Stoner was sitting musing about the family problems, feeling everything was hopeless, but then he sprang up from the chair and hobbled over to the window. He stood there staring out at the sun setting behind the pines across the field, marking the ending of yet another day he had stood by and done nothing to try to prove his son's innocence. What kind of father was he? He began to question himself. Why had he let all this time go by, those never-ending hours that had reminded him every second, from sunup until sundown, that Ashley was wanted by the law for raping that white girl? Why had he not shouted to the world that his son was innocent? Anything, but something.

Then Stoner began to hear a little voice within himself, a small, soothing, reassuring voice. It said: *What could you have done? Lawyer Taylor is doing everything he can, has been since the day you and Mr. Peterson went to him after Ashley left. Trust the man. He freed you, didn't he?*

And something else, the voice said to Stoner. *All this talk about shouting to the world that your boy is innocent—shout for what? Everybody who knows Ashley knows he didn't do it. Stop blaming yourself, man. You've done all you can do.*

Stoner turned from the window, his face now showing a kind of solemn expression—though still terribly worried. While he sat watching Bessie put supper on the table it seemed to him that the lamp in the center of the table had suddenly begun to burn brighter. Then it dimmed again, the flame almost going out.

Robert and Hattie had welcomed Ashley with open arms. Robert looked at Ashley, frowning. "Man, who you think raped that girl?"

"I don't know," Ashley said. "I've been thinking about it, wondering." He considered for a moment, then said, "Maybe it was some white man, trying to punish the girl for going around with a Negro."

"What about Tom Willis?" Robert suggested." He swore he was gonna find some way to get you."

Ashley shook his head skeptically. "Frankly, I don't believe it could have been Tom. He seemed to drop his grudge toward me long before that happened; I didn't hear nothing else about him threatening to *get* me."

"That's because he's sly as shit," Robert said. "He'll make you think he's forgot something, then he'll slip up behind you in the dark and slit your throat."

"Could have been him," Ashley said.

"If it was a white man that done it, why would he steal your hat and leave it there?"

"Just so they would have a black man to pin it on right away," Ashley said.

"I still think it was Tom Willis," Robert said.

"Could've been," Ashley said. "But whoever it was ain't gonna confess. I aim to find out who it was." He looked at Robert. "With your help, of course. Since I'll have to stay out of sight, you'll have to be my leg man."

Ashley was still the man wanted by the law. There wasn't much he could do to gather the information he needed to try to figure out who had attacked Mary Jo Rucker. He had to rely on Robert to do the nosing around in Mason. Ashley gave Robert the instructions, and Robert slipped in and out of crowds, drinking with the well-known hellers, spending time with the whores, and then bringing whatever he learned back to Ashley. And he didn't learn much that was of help.

Ashley had slipped home to see his family practically every night after dark, and he and Daisy had been seeing each other whenever Robert brought Daisy to his house.

Early on a Saturday morning Robert slipped Daisy to his house to visit with Ashley before the place got crowded.

Ashley and Daisy were sitting on the bed in Ashley's room, their arms around each other, talking, when Ashley mentioned Tom Willis.

"At least Tom Willis don't come in the cafe pestering me no more," Daisy said. "He hasn't been in there since that girl got raped."

Ashley turned and gave Daisy a long look. "What did you say? When did Tom Willis ever pester you?"

"Every time he'd come in the cafe—after me and you started going together."

"You didn't say anything to me about it," Ashley said accusingly.

"That's because I didn't want to worry you," Daisy admitted.

"What'd he do?"

"Just said a lot of stuff—you know—wanted to talk to me—take me home when I got off work. Then when I told him my daddy picked me up every night, he got mad and said it was my daddy that picked me up, all right—it was that so-and-so Ashley Brooks. He said he was gonna fix your...you know what."

Just then Robert tapped on the door and told Daisy it was time to leave. Daisy kissed Ashley and left him sitting on the edge of the bed staring thoughtfully at the floor.

When Robert got back, Ashley said to him, "It *was* Tom Willis."

"What made you change your mind?" Robert asked.

Ashley told him what Daisy had said, and Robert said, "Goddamned if he didn't fix your ass, too!"

"I ought to go find him right now and beat the goddamned shit out of him!" Ashley said, pacing the floor, furious.

"Wait a minute now, Ashley," Robert said, seeing how angry Ashley was. "You got to be careful about this. Let's go talk to that lawyer, Mr. Taylor."

They disguised themselves and left.

"Now ain't this a damn shame!" Ashley said. He and Robert were standing at the door of Moses Taylor's office, reading the sign tacked on the door stating that Taylor would be out of town for a few days.

"What do we do now?" Robert asked.

"Ashley, standing with his arms akimbo, his face crumpled with anger, said, "I don't know. I'm tired of this shit! I ain't hiding no damn more!"

"You rather be hanging from a tree by your neck?" Robert asked.

Late that Sunday evening Ashley went to see his family before it got dark. He told them what Daisy had said.

"I kept wondering about Tom Willis," Stoner said.

"Something told me it could've been him." He looked at Ashley. "We can't do nothing until Mr. Taylor comes back."

"Yes, I can," Ashley said. "I can go beat on his ugly head until he admits he did it!"

The Protectors hung out at an old dilapidated house far back in the woods where no one except them had any reason to go or ever thought of going. They had cleared a path to the ivy-covered house, swept down the cobwebs from the walls of one of the rooms, and slapped on some paint. They had moved in a few pieces of broken-down furniture and installed a wood stove, calling this their home away from home, where they could drink their whiskey in peace and plan their "protection" of the whites by taking the law into their own hands and punishing blacks for what the Protectors believed were their wrongdoings.

Thomas Rucker's three counterparts were Tater Mills, Lug Lawson, and Jake Jacobson.

Jake Jacobson was the meanest of the three, just as mean as Thomas Rucker, or meaner. Jake was still hoping to get revenge for an eye he lost in a fight with a black man, when the man had caught Jake raping his wife. Jake was middle-aged and undernourished-looking, and wore a black patch over his badly scarred eye socket.

Lug Lawson was a giant of a man, with blond, stubbly hair. His wife had run off with a black man and they were living up north. Lug couldn't stand the sight of a black man.

Tater Mills was the weakest of the Protectors. He

wanted out, said he was too old for their kind of violence. Tater was white-haired and fragile-looking,
with sunken cheeks. He had told the Protectors he
would have nothing to do with killings.

And they *were* killers; they had kidnapped a young
black boy a couple of months ago and taken him to
their hideout and tied him up and left him in the
unheated house, where he froze to death.

The fifteen-year-old boy had been found having sex
with the fourteen-year-old daughter of an overseer,
and the overseer had immediately called upon the
Protectors to punish the boy in order to keep his own
hands clean.

The boy was on his way home from work one night
when the Protectors seized him. He was still considered *missing*, and his elderly grandmother who raised
him had grieved herself to death in the meantime.

They had watched Jake carry the frozen-stiff body
over his shoulder out the door and bury it. And the
atmosphere of the house still hung heavy with the
memory of death.

Now it was inevitable that death would soon come
again in the old house, because Ashley Brooks had
been spotted running across the field to his family's
house late that Sunday evening.

Lug Lawson had been the last one assigned to hide
in the woods and keep watch over the Brooks home,
and when he spotted Ashley slipping across the field,
he nearly went crazy with exultation and burnt the
motor out of the old truck racing back to the old house
to tell the others.

They were celebrating their victory now, and

Thomas Rucker was already half drunk. He crashed a fist against the table where they all sat drinking, rattling the glasses on the table and nearly overturning the jar of white moonshine.

"We'll have to get to him before the sheriff does, so nobody will ever know we got him!" Thomas Rucker said. He took a big swallow of whiskey and, frowning, wiped his lips with the back of his hand.

Staring wide-eyed at Thomas Rucker, Tater said, "You mean you gonna bring him here?"

"That's exactly what he means," Jake snapped, the string on his eyepatch cutting into the red flesh on the side of his face. "That nigger needs to be taught a lesson—a agonizing lesson!"

"I'll have no part of it," Tater said, and he jumped up from the table, went to the window, and stood looking out toward the woods. The sun was sinking below the trees, the sky a brilliant, reddish orange, and Tater stood there looking out until darkness engulfed the old house.

Thomas Rucker pushed himself up from the table, lit the kerosene lamp in the center of the table, and sat back down. He poured himself another drink, because he knew what Tater was thinking.

"Come on over here, Tater, and join us and stop thinking about that nigger," Rucker said.

Tater went back and sat down. Looking around at the faces of the men at the table, shadowed by the dull lamplight, Tater thought they all looked like hollow-eyed dead men. He imagined himself running through the woods, running away from it all, but he knew his old legs couldn't outrun Jake's shotgun.

Thomas Rucker was staring at Tater out of the corner of his eye. "Hey, old man, you been mighty jumpy lately. You wouldn't be turning chicken on us, would you?"

Tater didn't answer, only stared at the flame in the lamp.

"Would you?" Thomas Rucker demanded an answer, but Tater didn't speak. "Well you just remember this, old man. You're a murderer just like we are. You're in too deep now to try to weasel your way out. If they get us they'll get you. You just remember that!" He slid the whiskey jar across the table to Tater. "Pour yourself a drink now and let's finish celebrating. We're going to have ourselves a real good time. And before long, I hope Jake will bring us back a little black visitor.

Tater had himself a first, a second, and a third drink, hoping the white lightning would make him forget what Thomas Rucker was planning.

Ashley stood at the mirror in Robert's house, brushing his hair and talking to Robert, who was sitting at the foot of the bed.

"Man, you better be careful out there when you slip home," Robert said. "Somebody might've already seen you."

"I am careful," Ashley said. "I wouldn't even go tonight, 'cept Mama and Daddy are over there thinking I'm dead or something."

Ashley was waiting around for it to get dark. He finished brushing his hair and walked over to the window and stood looking out at the sunset, a brilliant reddish orange.

"I love a sunset, man," he said to Robert. "It does something to me. Makes me feel all sad inside." He sighed, then said, "Well, in a minute I'll be out there on the run again, like a fugitive."

"Hey," Robert said. "Don't worry, man. That lawyer be back any time now." He looked straight at Ashley. "Want me to go with you?"

"Naw, man," Ashley said. "I'll be all right."

On his way home through the cornfield, Ashley kept glancing in all directions and straining his ears for any sound of movement that wasn't his. It was so dark he couldn't see his hand before his eyes. He squelched his fear by thinking of Daisy, how she had cried, warning him not to leave Robert's house again until he was cleared of the charges.

As Ashley hurried along, his imagination began to run away with him. He began to hear odd sounds behind him, like someone sneaking up behind him, cracking cornstalks under their feet. He turned and, seeing only blackness, told himself the noise had been the wind.

Cornstalks cracked again and Ashley wheeled around, catching the stunning blow to the side of his head. He moaned and felt the ground come up and smash against his face. He lay struggling to get up but he couldn't move a muscle. He felt himself slip- ping into unconsciousness and, moaning low, he fell silent and lay motionless on the ground.

"He's out cold," Jake said to Lug, after Jake had slammed the baseball bat against Ashley's head.

"We'd better tie him up," Jake said, "because when

that strong buck comes to he's bound to give us a hel-
luva time."

Ashley moaned as he regained consciousness for a
few seconds, feeling himself being dragged along by
the collar by the two men on either side of him. His
hands and feet were bound fast and he felt a warm
liquid running down the side of his face and neck and
on down his collar. He could faintly hear Daisy saying, "Something's going to happen! Something's
going to happen! Something's going to happen!"
Ashley's head dropped again, and again he fell into
unconsciousness.

Jake and Lug dragged Ashley's limp body to the
old truck parked out of sight back down the road, and
without mercy Ashley was thrown into the back of
the truck like the deer Jake had hunted down and
thrown there, bleeding and dying.

Annie hadn't felt well the whole week and had been
in bed most of the time. Mae had come over that
Sunday evening to fix dinner for her. They were in
the kitchen when Annie suddenly slumped to the floor
and couldn't get up. Mae struggled and got Annie to
bed, knowing she needed a doctor. Mae hoped one of
the boys would soon come home so she could send
for the doctor.

Frightened for Annie, Mae began to pace the floor
from Annie's bed to the front room window.

Annie had a livid complexion and could hardly talk
above a whisper. Mae was standing over the bed holding her hand and telling her she would have to leave
her alone and go for help, when she noticed Annie

motioning her to stoop down so she could tell her something.

Mae bent over and put her ear next to Annie's mouth.

"I can't go to my grave with this on my conscience," Annie whispered to Mae. "It was Tom, Mae. It was Tom that raped that white girl." Annie's voice seemed to grow a little stronger. "Tom come in that night with all them bloody scratches on his face, and I asked him what had happened. He said he'd been in a fight. Next day I heard tell of that girl being raped. Then I began to wonder, but I didn't say anything to Tom."

Annie's voice weakened again, and Mae squeezed her hand. Then Annie got her breath back again. "Tom was drunk the other night. I told him it sure was bad about Stoner and Bessie's boy having to run off and hide like that, when everybody knowed he didn't rape that girl. Tom laughed and said he fixed that Ashley Brooks good when he left his hat in the barn. I stared at Tom and started crying. 'Tom, did you rape that girl?' I asked him. He didn't say nothing else. But I know it was him, Mae."

Annie stopped talking and lay with her eyes walled back. Mae began smoothing Annie's gray and white hair back and calling her.

"Can you hear me, Annie?"

Annie didn't answer. Mae put her lips to Annie's ear. "I'm going to get help, Annie, honey. I'll be back as soon as I can."

Mae ran up to their bossman's house to get him to take Annie to the doctor. When they got back to

Annie's house Mae jumped out of the car and ran
inside. She found Annie still staring at the ceiling.
Dead!

Late that evening Mae rapped on Stoner and
Bessie's door. She told them what Annie had told her.
Stoner grabbed his hat and hurried off to Peterson's
house. Peterson called Mr. Brinkley to find out how
to get in touch with Mr. Taylor in New York. Moses
Taylor told him he would be back there the next day.

When Stoner and Mae Willis got to Mr. Taylor's
office the next day, he was there as promised. Mae
told him everything. Moses Taylor wasted no time in
having Tom Willis arrested. Tom Willis confessed.

Chapter 17

Ashley lay motionless on the dingy mattress and pillow on the cot, his eyes still closed and his hands still bound together behind his back. The right side of the pillow and Ashley's right shoulder were soaked with blood.

"He's dead!" Tater said nervously, ready to panic.

"He ain't dead," Thomas Rucker said. "Not yet. I have a little business to transact with him first." Thomas Rucker got up and walked over to where Ashley lay unconscious on his back. "Untie his hands, Jake," he said.

Jake went over and untied Ashley's hands.

"Good," Thomas Rucker said. "Now let's all sit back and wait. I want to see the expression on his face when he comes to and sees us."

"He's been unconscious ever since you brought him

in last night," Tater said. "You sure he ain't dead?"

Thomas Rucker looked around at Tater, then walked up to him and squeezed his cheeks together. "Stop worrying, old man. He'll be around soon." He chuckled. "But if that black nigger knowed what I have planned for him he'd die right now and save himself some misery."

Ashley slowly opened his eyes, his gaze following the zigzagged crack in the ceiling. The awful pain and the loud roaring in his head prevented him from being aware of the silence in the room, where over at the table his four captors sat breathless, watching him.

Ashley's eyes gradually found the four men staring in his direction. His vision was blurred and he kept opening and closing his eyes, trying to make out the faces.

The first face that came into focus was that of Thomas Rucker. Ashley let his shoulders fall back to the bed and closed his eyes in despair. He knew now why he had been kidnapped!

Thomas Rucker, a smirk on his face, walked up to the cot and stood over Ashley. "You know why you're here, don't you, boy?"

Ashley ran the tip of his fingers up the side of his head until they touched the bloody, throbbing lump; a greasy salve rubbed off on his hand. (Tater had dressed Ashley's wound when no one was watching, the night they brought Ashley in.)

Ashley slowly raised his head and looked at his bloody shoulder; then he looked around at the faces glaring at him and dropped his head back on the pillow, holding his head and moaning with pain.

"Yeah, he knows why he's here," Rucker said. He bent over closer to Ashley, who was lying with his eyes closed, refusing to give Thomas Rucker the satisfaction of knowing just how frightened he was.

"You know why we brought you here, too, doncha boy?" Rucker said again, more strongly.

Ashley lay silent, his eyes closed.

"Well, you don't have to say nothing if you don't want to," Thomas Rucker said. "You just lay there and listen. You see, we're gonna give you a little trial for what you done to my daughter, sonny boy. Yessiree, we're gonna give you our own little trial. Of course, we already know you're guilty. We just want to hear what you got to say to defend yourself…, not that it'll do you any good…, but we'll listen…, you know, like down at the courthouse…, where the jury listens to the evidence. Then, after you're found guilty, we're gonna punish you for the crime…, *just* the way you oughta *be* punished."

Ashley felt warm blood trickling from his wound. He felt dizzy and nauseated and the room began to spin around. He lay motionless on the cot.

"He needs some food in his belly," Tater said. "That's why he keeps passing out."

"Shut up, old man," Jake said. "He don't need nothing but killing!" He adjusted the black patch over his eye.

A fire crackled in the wood stove, a pot of soup sat heating on top, and some cheese and weiners and crackers lay on the table. The Protectors were getting ready to have lunch.

They took turns guarding Ashley that night. Rucker and Lug and Jake left Tater and Ashley alone long enough for Tater to slip Ashley a bowl of soup and some crackers. Then Rucker and Lug had left the shack telling Ashley his "trial" would be the next morning. While Jake and Tater sat at the table playing cards, Jake began to nod off drowsily.

Ashley lay motionless on the cot watching Jake dozing, then jerking his head back up. Ashley had been fully conscious all day and the wound had finally stopped bleeding. He knew he had to find a way out of there before morning; he wouldn't stand a chance at that trial.

Jake finally lowered his head to the table and it remained there. He began to snore. Ashley immediately focused on Tater's gaunt face. Tater refused to look Ashley's way because he was deathly afraid of Jake. Ashley began to whisper to Tater, trying to get him to come over beside him. Tater finally got up enough nerve to go over to Ashley.

"Help me, man," Ashley pleaded. "You know what they're gonna do to me tomorrow. Please! Help me get away from here," he whispered.

"They'll kill me!" Tater whispered back to Ashley.

"You come go with me!" Ashley said. "Come on, help me. Untie my hands. We don't have much time. The other two will be back soon. Please, man. You don't want to be part of no lynching. I can tell you ain't like them."

Tater glanced over at a loudly snoring Jake, and his trembling fingers began to untie Ashley's hands.

Ashley closed his eyes, deeply relieved, as Tater

fumbled at the tight knot. His head was spinning
something awful, and when his hands were free he
tried to stand up but kept plopping back down on the
bed.

With his eyes glued to Jake's head on the table,
Tater helped Ashley up from the bed and to the door.
Then Ashley and Tater disappeared into the dark
woods.

Jake sat straight up in the chair and looked around.
His eyes stopped on the empty cot. He jumped up and
ran to the door and looked around. "Tater? Tater?"
Jake ran and got his shotgun and stormed out the door.

Ashley and Tater had stumbled deep into the
woods. Tater had grown too tired to help Ashley, and
now Ashley was helping Tater along, feeling warm
blood start to trlckle from his wound again. Then his
knees buckled under him and they fell to the ground,
he in one direction and Tater in the other. They raised
up and sat side by side against a tree, panting for
breath. Ashley stood up and pulled Tater to his feet.
"We got to keep going, man."

"Do you know where we are?" Tater asked Ashley,
out of breath, trying desperately to keep from collapsing to the ground.

"I'm not sure," Ashley said, stopping and looking
around. "Let me think for a minute." Then Ashley said
excitedly, "I think I know where we are. I think there's
a clearing straight over that way that leads to the old
Sandy Fork Road. If it does we're in business. I know
a place not far from there where we can hide."

Ashley had recognized that area of the woods from

the many hunting trips he had been on with Stoner
and some others. They reached the clearing and were
now able to move faster because there were no trees
to duck, just entangled underbrush.

"Come on, man," Ashley said to Tater, far behind
him. "We got it made now." He ran back and took
Tater by the arm.

The weatherbeaten cabin sat on a hill hidden back
in the trees. Ashley let Tater walk on his own now,
running ahead and rapping on the door.

"Who is it?" an old man's voice called from behind
the door.

"It's Ashley, Sam! Open the door quick!"

Ashley heard Sam opening the door, muttering to
himself, "Ashley! Ashley!"

Sam hadn't seen Ashley or Stoner since the day of
Stoner's trial, but he kept abreast of what was going
on in the community by visiting the general store far
down the road.

"Ashley! You son of a gun! Come on in!" Then
Sam spotted the white man standing behind Ashley
and his eyes peeled.

"It's all right, Sam," Ashley said. "Let us in." Sam
stood back and Ashley rushed inside, Tater behind
him. Sam bolted the door and leaned his old shotgun
up beside it.

Chapter 18

Rucker and Lug had driven up and found Jake running out of the woods with the shotgun. When Jake told them what had happened, they joined Jake in the search. They scoured the surrounding woods late into the night, with no success. Finally they went stumbling back to the old house exhausted.

The three of them sat at the table now, looking at the bloodstained pillow on the empty cot.

"You know what that means, don't you, boys?" Thomas Rucker said. "If they get to the right authorities and tell them what happened, they'll be coming after us. And you know what else we got hanging over our heads; you better know old Tater is going to spill his guts about that boy." Rucker poured himself another drink and swallowed it. "We should've got rid of Tater right after that boy died. He's been running around scared to death ever since it happened."

Rucker got up from the table and began to pace the floor. "We got to find them. Quick!"

The news that Ashley Brooks was missing spread fast. Tom Willis was behind bars awaiting trial for the rape of Mary Jo Rucker, but Moses Taylor didn't know if Thomas Rucker had heard the news. Rucker hadn't been around since the arrest . He was missing, just like Ashley was. It was possible he didn't know who had raped his daughter—or didn't even care, as long as he made some black man pay for it. Preferably a black man he already had it in for.

After Robert had come over to tell her that Ashley was missing, Daisy Lane had sat up and cried all night, worrying about what had happened to him. In the morning, she didn't feel like going to work. She sat with Robert talking about everything that had happened, searching for some clue as to where Ashley might be, afraid even to consider the possibilty that he might be dead.

Robert was just as worried as Daisy; he kept blaming himself for letting Ashley go out alone.

Ashley stood in Sam's cabin, holding back the dingy little curtain and looking out of the window at the surrounding woods.

It was the day after Ashley and Tater had arrived at Sam's cabin and Sam had attended to Ashley's head wound. Sam had also heated up a pot of navy beans and brought out a stack of baked sweet potatoes and fed them. Then he had spread some old quilts on the floor and, totally exhausted from running, Ashley and Tater had dropped down on them and slept like babies.

By sunset that day and Ashley was still pacing the floor and worrying and peeping out the window, expecting to see Rucker and the Protectors, as he had been doing all day. He had a bandage made from a strip of white sheet around his head, and Sam had given him one of his old shirts to wear.

"They're out there somewhere looking for us," Ashley said. He turned to Sam. "I'm scared for my family, Mr. Sam. No telling what them crazy men might do. If they hurt one of my sisters...."

Ashley paused, obviously torn apart inside, not knowing which way to turn. A sudden wind cracked the old house and swayed the forest treetops. Tater, who had been quiet since their arrival, hurried over to the window and peered down toward the woods again.

Ashley resumed pacing, rubbing his palms together. He stopped suddenly and stared at the floor, massaging his forehead, as if it would help him to think. "I've got to get over to Mr. Peterson's before dark," he said finally, looking over at Tater. "Mr. Tater, I'll tell Mr. Peterson to send the sheriff over here to get you...."

Tater looked frightened, as if he didn't want Ashley to leave him. Then he cleared his throat. "Go on. Do what you have to do, son. Don't worry about me. My life ain't worth a nickel no more."

Sam stared at Ashley, his eyes clouded, his chin trembling. "They might shoot you down like a dog, Ashley. It's too dangerous for you to go out there."

"I don't have no other choice," Ashley said, checking out the window again, thinking Thomas Rucker could have somebody watching Sam's house. "It's driving me crazy staying here and doing nothing."

When Ashley struck out through the woods to Mr. Peterson's house, the sun was still up. He fought his way through briars and mud, his wound aching something awful, his heart in his throat at the least rustle of the trees around him.

John Peterson was greatly relieved when he answered the knock at his door and found Ashley standing there. It didn't matter that the young man had a bandage around his head and that there was blood and mud caked on his shoes. What mattered was that Ashley was alive. He had heard that Tom Willis had confessed to the rape of the Rucker girl and that the search for Ashley had changed to one concerned about his safety.

After Ashley told him everything, Peterson said, "I'll call Sheriff Wendy." And he headed for the telephone .

Ashley stopped him. "Mr. Peterson, don't tell him where I am. Just tell him where Mr. Tater is. Tell him to go over to Mr. Sam's house, in case some of them go there looking for me and try to hurt Mr. Sam or Mr. Tater."

Peterson thought about it a minute. "You know, Ashley, everybody knows Sheriff Wendy is not a very nice man, but he is still the law. He'll put a stop to the KKK or the Protectors, or any other group that makes trouble in the county. He surely knows that a mob action would be not only an interference with his duty but an actual insult. There are a lot of more reasonable whites around here, too, who try to prevent violence wherever they can, son. And Wendy has to answer to them as well as to the rotten apples."

Ashley held Mr. Peterson's gaze. "Still, I want to talk to Mr. Taylor first," Ashley said. "And if you don't mind, Mr. Peterson, please take me by home. I know Mama and Daddy are going out of their minds with worry."

Bessie fell on her knees and thanked God that her son was alive, and Stoner, his eyes welling with tears, grabbed his jacket to go with Ashley and Mr. Peterson to find Mr. Taylor.

Peterson wasn't taking any chances. He had his old shotgun in the truck as he and Ashley and Stoner sped into town to locate Taylor. They found him in his office on the telephone. All day he had been by the phone in case some of the men searching for Ashley should try to call him.

Mr. Taylor contacted the sheriff immediately, and Ashley told him everything that had happened since the day Mr. Snellings had rushed up to his house to tell him that Mary Jo Rucker had been raped and that his cap had been found at the scene.

Ashley was surprised to learn that Tom Willis was already in jail and had confessed to the rape. Sheriff Wendy's deputies were still looking for Thomas Rucker and Lug and Jake. They had gone to Sam's house, taken Tater into custody, and put Sam in a safe place until Rucker and his men were arrested.

They found Rucker and Lug and Jake in another county, on the run.

After it was all settled that Ashley was no longer wanted by the sheriff and that his name was entirely cleared, he sat in Mr. Taylor's office with Stoner and Bessie and Daisy Lane. "I think this calls for a celebration," Ashley said.

Mr. Taylor smiled and shook his head. "There isn't time," he said.

Ashley was puzzled. "What do you mean?"

"One of the reasons I've been trying so hard to find you," Mr. Taylor said, "is to get you to the college before it's too late. They'll only hold your registration a couple more days, even with me using all my influence."

"Then what are we sitting here for?" Stoner asked. "Let's get home and get those bags packed again. The celebrating can wait."

Epilogue

July 21st, 1946. It was a beautiful summer day. It was the last day of lawyer Ashley Brooks's visit back home with his family.

Ashley lay out under the old shade tree in the backyard. Out by the packhouse at the edge of the cornfield sat the old pickup that Peterson had loaned him and eventually given to him so he could come home to see family and friends when he was on breaks while in college and law school. The old truck, discarded and coated with rust, brought back a lot of memories for Ashley.

Earlier he had sidled up to it, opened the rusty old door, slid under the steering wheel, and sat lost in thought.

Now Ashley lay relaxing in the cool shade of the tree, relaxing, not eager to get back to his law practice in New York. He glanced out at the field of tall, waving corn; he could almost see himself barefoot in the soil, pushing the plow and saying "get up" to the mule.

The plush green grass he rested on was comforting, and he lay staring at the bright blue sky, the clouds floating lazily along, alleging all was right with the world. He had made it—reached for that unreachable star and grasped it. All the Thomas Ruckers and Sheriff Wendys of the world had not kept him from obtaining his dream.

Just then the back screen door opened and Daisy hurried out to spread a soft blue blanket beside Ashley and lay their infant son on it. She kissed her husband and told him she had lots to do, helping Bessie and Minnie and Eva with the going-away dinner.

Ashley reached over, lifted the baby, and set him on his chest. The baby cooed and Ashley raised his head up and kissed him on his little face, then laid his head back down and returned to gazing up at the sky.

"How many times through the years have I poured out my troubles to you?" Ashley whispered. "And like Grandma said; you always listened. Now I've got everything a man could possibly want, but something is missing, living and working up there in New York. I think you know what it is without my having to tell you. I always intended to practice law among my own people. It was something I promised myself. I've got to come home again."

MARY MCLEOD BETHUNE
EDUCATOR
By Bernice Anderson Poole

Born in 1875 in South Carolina, Mary Jane McLeod was considered a special child from the very beginning. She dreamed of doing things that seemed impossible for rural blacks at the time, such things as learning to read and write. In 1887 when she was offered a scholarship to attend Scotia Seminary in Concord, North Carolina, she eagerly accept-

ed, going on from there to the Moody Bible Institute in Chicago. She returned to the South to teach. After marrying a fellow teacher, Albertus Bethune. Mrs. Bethune established her own school in Daytona, Florida, in 1904, merging it in 1923 with the Cookman Institute to form Bethune-Cookman Collegiate Institute Among other acomplishments, she founded the National Council of Negro Women.

A Melrose Square Book

HOLLOWAY HOUSE PUBLISHING COMPANY
8060 Melrose Avenue, Los Angeles, CA 90046

ABOUT THE AUTHOR

Bernice Anderson Poole is a native of North Carolina and has lived all of her life in the South, in both North Carolina and Virginia. Her great passion is writing about the country South, the kind of atmosphere she grew up in. She is the author of a biography published by Melrose Square, *Mary McLeod Bethune: Educator*, and of a young adult novel, *The Haunted Woods*, published by Scholastic Press. She has also written numerous short stories and articles for magazines.